# STEARN'S BREAK

Looking to start a new life, away from the futility of working an exhausted gold mine, Will Stearn and his partner Clem Tapper ride to Ragland. On the way, they encounter Connie Boe and her wounded driver, and stop to assist. Accepting Connie's offer of paying them to ride shotgun and guard her wagon the rest of the journey, Will and Clem travel on with the others. But when they reach Ragland, they'll find that the town is tough . . .

CALEB RAND

# STEARN'S BREAK

*Complete and Unabridged*

**LINFORD**
*Leicester*

First published in Great Britain in 2014 by
Robert Hale Limited
London

First Linford Edition
published 2017
by arrangement with
Robert Hale
an imprint of
The Crowood Press
Wiltshire

A catalogue record for this book is available
from the British Library.

ISBN 978–1–4448–3489–5

Published by
F. A. Thorpe (Publishing)
Anstey, Leicestershire

Set by Words & Graphics Ltd.
Anstey, Leicestershire
Printed and bound in Great Britain by
T. J. International Ltd., Padstow, Cornwall

This book is printed on acid-free paper

# 1

At sundown, Will Stearn was catching the last heat of the day. He was leaning on the handle of a shovel, thoughtfully looking around him.

The land was turning red and gold with the last burst of light. The soft ridge winds blew warm across the remnants of the old mine, and broken, weather-warped timbers highlighted a scene of desolation. The silence was interminable and there was no movement except for thin clouds of shifting dust. High above the ruins of what had once been a working pit, a buzzard searched for carrion. It cawed with disappointment, circling, until with a final flap of broad wings it flew off to richer territory.

Tall, pared lean to fitness by hard work, Will was now losing interest, distancing himself from a reminder of better days. On hearing movement from within the mine shaft, he turned to see the crooked frame of a man emerging from the gloomy, yard-wide opening.

Clem Tapper was a man close on sixty years of age. He was wirily built, strength was still evident in the muscles of his arms, but there was a tiredness etched into his weather-worn features.

Tapper struggled out of the mine, bracing himself against the surge of heat. Dirt covered him, blotching his face, darkening the greyness of his range shirt. He lifted one hand to his face and rubbed at his sunken eyes, breathed a deep sigh of submission.

'Still nothing?' Will said, but more of a statement than a question.

Tapper lifted his head and his eyes searched through the glare of the day. He saw his friend standing amongst the clutter of old timber and heaped clay, and shook his head. 'I went in more'n fifty feet, Will.'

'It's nothing more than a big goddamn gopher hole,' Will said, and dropped the shovel at his feet. He walked slowly across to the entrance of the mine shaft, working a slight cramp out of his shoulders. He knew that Clem was watching him closely, and he continued looking about him, making no attempt to disguise his indifference. He had known Clem for most of his thirty years, and in that time had seen him change from a confident, carefree man, to someone who had lost his keenness, now desperately struggling through life seeking ever more unworkable schemes.

'It's there, Will, I know it. A couple more days an' I'll bring out enough gold to set us up for life. You see if I don't. I'll buy you them brood mares you've always wanted, maybe a business in town.' Tapper's rheumy eyes glistened as he dreamed his way from looming failure. Weary though he was from long hours of digging at fruitless earth, his spirit continued doggedly. He shifted across to his friend and went on eagerly. 'Gimme another week. I can see it, smell it, touch it. It's like a game o' hide an' seek.'

Will studied him calmly for a long moment and Tapper shifted away as if hurt by the cool scrutiny.

'Three months, Clem. That was the limit. That's what we agreed on,' Will said.

'Yeah, I know. But what's three or four months when you're seekin' a lifetime's riches?'

Will shook his head slowly. 'It's what we agreed.'

Tapper backed off further, stood regarding Will with a measure of antagonism. 'So you want to pull out? Is that what you're sayin'?'

Will nodded. 'If we stay another night, we'll stay another day. So let's go now, while there's enough daylight to pack. We'll travel through the night, rest up in the river country tomorrow. Then we'll push on to Ragland.'

Tapper lifted his chin. A stubborn line of muscle braced his jaw, and argument flared in his grey eyes. 'I came for gold, Will, an' hell I'm goin' to get it. That's with you or on my own.'

Again, Will shook his head. 'Listen to me, Clem. If you're on your own, you won't last another week. You've had your chance. You paid a hundred dollars for a hole in the ground . . . nothing more. Besides, we're out of grub. Let's get packed.'

Tapper looked more sour now, the colour draining from his craggy features. 'You're a disappointment, Will. You ain't got no stick.'

The words hung heavily between them, and as soon as he spoke, Tapper knew he had made a mistake. Never before had he allowed himself even to mildly slate the young man who had ridden many trails with him, uncomplaining, having him make most of their decisions.

'I had it in Leadville, when you grubstaked us for trapping up on the snowline and we near froze,' Will retorted. 'And again when we sat starving outside of that Blanco Trading Post you said was the next Garden of

Eden. I stayed on to let you get roostered in Durango, and lose our stake in a hand of cooncan. Hell, I've stuck around for so many stupid reasons, that some of it's rubbing off on me. Well, I've had enough. So, let's get moving while there's light.'

Tapper trembled with doubt, standing uneasily under Will's determined look. He had such high hopes for success, but now the acrid taste of another failure filled his mouth.

'You got no right to tell me what to do, Will. If I want to stay, I'll stay. You can ride off if you want.'

Will took in a deep breath. He kept his lips tight, holding back. He kicked the shovel away, watching for a moment as it clattered into the rubble he had been clearing. He reached for a small bag that hung from a corner of the cross timber above the mine entrance, pulled it down and tossed it to Tapper.

'That's about a hundred dollars' worth of gold dust,' he said. 'Three months gravel for two. That's not much more than fifty cents a day, each. For God's sake Clem, what we eat's more than double that. We're going behind faster than a mole eats worms. Think about it for a few minutes.'

Will walked down the squat hill towards his tent. He fetched out his war sack, rolled it up and tied it behind his saddle. Next, he pulled down his tent and slung it across the back of his sorrel mare. 'I'm taking no more than what I came with,' he muttered. 'Next to goddamn nothing.' Then he grabbed up a pick and a shovel and secured them beneath the flap of his saddle-bag. Finally he pulled his gunbelt from the tent pole, and buckled it determinedly around his waist.

Tapper stood in the day's dwindling warmth, watching, a frown crumpling his brow. When Will mounted his horse and pulled the reins into his grip, he drove his own shovel into the ground, reeled off a string of curses. He went and dragged his own tent down, hastily and untidily sorting his gear. Then he saddled his claybank, slinging and tying-in two gunny-sacks behind. He climbed wearily on to his mount, and after a sullen look around, he spat a thin line of watery brown ooze towards the mine entrance. 'Didn't need him to tell me all that,' he griped, before turning his back on the site.

Will moved off down the trail. He knew from past experience that Tapper would want to follow on his own, and probably for two or three hours. He also knew that when they made camp next morning, they could rest up, hang for trout, and the old timer's resentment would ease. Twenty-four hours on, and Clem Tapper would be ready and eager to tackle another hair-brained scheme.

# 2

'We've still got *some* dollars left,' Will said. 'With the gold, it should make up to nearly four hundred. I'll take fifty and what's left should be enough for a down payment.'

'What down payment? What're you talkin' about?'

'Somewhere for you. You always said one day you'd do more than dig dust, and now's the chance. Ragland's wide open, ripe and ready for more than beaneries and mughouses.'

'So I compete by openin' up another one?'

'No. It would be a place of fine fixings. You'd get to know the right people, not crooks and drifters. You'll get a hell of a lot of satisfaction seeing them roll their eyes when they've eaten at one of *your* tables. I'll wager that's a rare look.'

Tapper straightened away from the fire where he had been kneeling to cook two small trout. His face was wreathed in smoke for a moment and he coughed, gave a choking laugh. 'Huh. Maybe I could try some o' these little fellers stuffed with wild onions,' he suggested with a wry grin.

'Yeah, maybe you could,' Will encouraged. 'Think on. You said yourself that they're canning just about everything, nowadays . . . turtle soup . . . lobster? Where'd we read you can pack just about anything in ice or salt?'

'Canon City. It was Canon City. But if we got a few hundred dollars, why not a split down the middle? It's always been our way.'

'Yeah, but not this time, Clem. You're going to be on your own . . . for a bit, anyways.'

Tapper gaped at him. 'An' that's what you'll be takin' the fifty for,' he accused. 'The getaway ticket. Well, let me tell you, young feller, until this ol' body goes belly up, *I go where you go*.'

Will went on unsaddling his horse. As he dropped his war sack to the ground, looking for a likely place to make his camp, he saw Tapper coming to confront him with more resentment. It had only been two hours since his old partner had drawn level with him on the trail, agreeing that the mine was worthless, most likely always had been.

Will held his hand up against the rising sun, thought he'd go for a different, more direct tactic. 'You're through drifting, Clem,' he said. 'I could see back at the mine. The only thing that drove you on was that goddamn fever, the craving to get rich. I know it was for me as much as for you, but I told Pa I'd look out for you for as long as it took. Well, that's now. Our trail forks in Ragland. Yours ends there.'

Gloom shadowed Tapper's old face. His shoulders bowed under Will's pronouncement. He knew, had already admitted to himself that he'd slowed up, that even camp chores were becoming harder to perform. But he wasn't yet ready to accept he was finished. 'You're steppin' out a mite too far, son,' he growled thickly. 'A man puts on some age, but it don't mean he's ready for pasture . . . or the glue factory.'

Will reached out, but Tapper withdrew with a quick backwards step, stood studying the young man dourly, wanting more reason.

'Clem, I've given it a lot of thought. Not much else recently, truth be told. I'm cutting out and you're staying in Ragland. Hell, it's not that bad an idea, and it'll be for the both of us. You can cook some of that fancy fare you're always talking about. When I get a dollar stake, I'll send it on and you can invest. At least we'll own something as partners. Huh, you'll soon be feeding the multitude. What do you say?'

Tapper licked his lips slowly. He knew that when Will made up his mind to do something, nothing much could budge him. 'You reckon these local folk are ready for pork an' apples . . . on the same plate?' he asked, but a little less doubtful.

'Yeah, I reckon. Make a change from goddamn beef and biscuits, swimming together.' Will was silent for a time, as though he was thinking of the food, then he gave a wistful smile. 'What was it that old Apache chief had us eat? Mountain oysters and blood pudding? 'Died an' gone to heaven', you said. You know what I'm saying makes sense, Clem.'

'I know the Army wants horses. Is that it, Will? You're runnin' after mustangs?'

'Maybe. Whatever it is, it's out there. But I'm being slowed down. The frontier's opening up and there's new opportunities. I'll do my share of making good by it. It's what Pa would have accepted, Clem.'

Tapper suddenly looked a lot less significant, more irrelevant in the scheme of things. He sniffed and turned slowly away.

Will was uneasy with himself for

having to do this to his partner, but he was right. He could travel lighter and faster on his own, change route quicker. He watched Tapper make his way back to the fire, and for the next hour, during and after they had made breakfast of the trout, they stayed reserved with their own thoughts. For Will's part, he was allowing Tapper another turn at getting used to a new future.

It was late afternoon when they broke camp, when Tapper nudged his clay-bank in close. 'I've thought it out,' he declared. 'It don't come natural, an' I don't like it, but I'll give your way a try. I could buy a freighter, convert it to bring stuff in from the east . . . fruit from California, maybe. I'd need more money, but you did say partners, didn't you? How long d'you reckon on bein' gone?'

'With your ideas for filling a plate . . . not long, Clem. And I'll always be wanting you as my partner. That'll never change.' Will grinned and nodded encouragement. After another short consideration of his friend's proposal, Tapper smiled in return.

They rode together down along the widening creek, enjoying the sweep of late evening breezes. With every mile, Tapper became less irritable and more positive about a life in Ragland. He knew the town was one of many that were just beginning to settle down after an initial taming. There was talk of a rail link, a spur dropping down from the Santa Fe Railroad and running parallel to the Rio Grande. A couple of saloons and boarding-houses had recently opened, and there was a cattleman's bank, and a town sheriff appointed to maintain civic order.

$\star$ $\star$ $\star$

After the rich colours of sundown, night settled quietly and calmly. Will Stearn and Clem Tapper rode through the hours of darkness, striking camp early the following day. They settled for a few hours, and in the afternoon, stayed with the run of the creek that would finally lead them into Ragland.

It was near to the end of another day when they reached a junction, a branched trail that broke east and west. Will drew rein, asked his old friend about the choice of routes.

'Goddamnit, Will, this country's so pretty an' peaceful, I could stay right here . . . get my legs wet with a little pannin',' Tapper said. 'An' just when I was comin' round to the idea o' settin' up shop. So to avoid temptation, let's ride the ridge trail. It's on risin' ground . . . gives us a chance to have a good look.'

For ten miles, they rode the more used, worn track. After that, they weaved through heavily timbered country, then they broke on to a rise, saw a run of hills behind which snugged the town of Ragland.

Having decided to make one last camp, they were about to unsaddle their horses, when they heard gunfire suddenly peppering the silence of the ridge. Will reined in quickly and turned about, was looking back along the trail as Tapper rode alongside.

'You hear that?' Tapper said. 'Was that gunfire?'

'Certainly weren't a woodpecker. There's some sort of vehicle, too. Being driven hard, sounds like.'

'The stage?' Tapper suggested, looking intently at his friend.

Will shook his head. 'No, not the stage.' He drew his horse in, looking around for the nearest cover. 'And I guess it's none of our business, either,' he added, pointing to a willow thicket at the edge of their clearing.

Tapper grunted an agreement but drew his old Colt. When he joined Will in the light timber, he hitched his horse, then retraced his steps to the clearing. He could see a turn about fifty yards away, back up the trail. 'Somebody's makin' trouble. So much for the goddamn peace,' he muttered.

Will didn't reply. He hadn't drawn

his own Colt, but he was tense and alert for more revealing sounds.

Tapper was satisfied that whatever was about to happen, they were ready and prepared. He knew that if trouble was headed their way, Will Stearn was more than capable of handling it. He stood quietly listening to the shooting that was getting closer by the minute. Then above the echo of the shots, he heard the unmistakeable crack of a bull whip, the wheeze and rattle of wheels rolling speedily towards them. For the next couple of minutes, he impatiently edged forward for a first sight.

'Don't go any further,' Will said quietly. 'We don't want to get drawn in until we know what's going on.'

Tapper offered a slight shrug, but he eased back. His eyes remained settled on the bend in the trail, his jaw hardening when a covered wagon veered into sight. The wagon was rocking dangerously from one side to the other, the driver crouching down on his seat, his right shoulder dipped as if he had been hit.

'It's one o' them goddamn mud wagons,' Tapper called out. 'Like hell with the hide off, an' the driver looks hurt.'

Will was looking to where the low, dying sun was highlighting the roil of dust and dirt. It wasn't until he saw the three men riding hard in the drag of the wagon with their guns blazing, that he gave instructions to Tapper.

'Let the riders come, Clem. When I say, throw as much lead as you can around them. But try and keep out of sight. We don't want them knowing there's just two of us.'

'Two against three, ain't exactly scary odds,' Tapper stated. Ready and willing to show his alliance with Will, he lifted his gun and kept an aim.

The wagon hurtled towards them, passing with a furious noise that shattered the calm of their surroundings.

'Now,' Will called and opened fire. His first shots ripped through the rising

19

clouds of dust behind the wagon. Tapper echoed Will's fire, and between them they kept up a persistent barrage, each reloading while the other fired. Eventually, the masked riders broke off their pursuit on the wagon. They retreated to near the turn in the trail, and one of them cursed, pulling a rifle from his saddle holster.

'Stay where you are, Clem,' Will shouted above the echoes of their gunshots. 'They're not sure who or where we are, yet.'

But Tapper, in his enthusiasm for a fight, hastily edged into the open again. A bullet cracked across his arm and he was thrown sideways and down, rolling out to the rutted trail.

Cursing him, Will left his own cover and ran forward. The three riders had grouped, were drawing close rein, trying to manage their horses' jitteriness.

Will showed himself, his only cover the dust which still hung in clouds beneath the trees. Uncertain whether

Tapper was dead, badly wounded or merely grazed, he cursed again and brought up his Colt. 'I guess we brought this on ourselves,' he hissed, and with a two-handed grip, coolly opened fire.

Will shot one of the riders. The man dropped forward in the saddle, his horse swinging away, breaking into a panicked run. The other two riders let loose a disorderly return of fire. It was a gesture of their resentment before they turned back the way they had come.

Will stood in the shelter of the dust cloud, muttering, as he reloaded his Colt. 'Never interfere with nothin' that don't bother you,' he said wryly. 'Who the hell said that?' he asked of no one in particular. When he was satisfied the riders had fled, he made his way back to his horse, grinned at seeing Tapper staggering back from the trail.

The old man was cursing with more than usual venom, ripping the sleeve from his tattered, grimy shirt. He pinched the flesh below his left elbow, dabbed at a flow of brownish blood. 'Bullet must have ricoched off something,' he gruffed. 'Wouldn't have caught me that easy.'

Will withdrew Tapper's hand and had a look at the wound. He ripped off a strip of old shirt and after washing the graze with some canteen water, bandaged the arm.

'Won't stop you flipping a beefsteak, Clem,' he said. 'You OK to ride?'

'Sure. I'll be needin' a couple o' new shirts, though. I might be too old to ride trail with you, but it didn't stop me helpin' to see off a bunch o' goddamn road agents.'

'That's right,' Will agreed and grinned. He stepped into his saddle and when Tapper had seated himself on his own horse, he turned down the trail. He looked ahead, listened carefully to the returning silence of the ridge, and wondered how the wagon driver had fared, where he'd got to. Figuring that they would make it to Ragland with one more night's ride, he settled into a slow easy pace.

# 3

Will Stearn was first to see the wagon. It was set against the big gnarled bole of a cottonwood near the toe of the foothills. He also saw a woman hurrying from the creek, water sloshing in a canvas bucket.

'They didn't get far. Driver must have been hit bad,' Clem Tapper said, reining in beside him. 'An' I didn't see *her.*'

'No. She was keeping real quiet,' Will granted and pushed forward. He set his horse into a jog, but before he got to within fifty feet, the woman stepped out from cover of the wagon. She was of striking appearance, of an age that carried lines from the corners of her eyes and mouth. Her figure was full and her unbefitting clothes were designed to set it off. She had a scattergun in her hands and it was aimed directly at Will's chest.

'Lower your piece, ma'am, we mean you no harm,' he said.

'And I mean you none, as long as you don't come any further,' the woman retorted.

As Will sat watching her, Tapper edged in closer behind him. 'I wouldn't push her,' he said. 'If she pulls the trigger o' that thing, any one of us could get taken out.'

Will smiled and removed his hat, brushed his hair back from his brow. He reached down and pulled his water canteen from the side of his saddle. With what looked like disregard for the situation, he slaked his thirst, wound the canteen string around the horn and let his horse walk on.

'I'm thinking you've got trouble enough without us giving you more,' he said. He was conscious that the shotgun was lowered a fraction, but the woman was obviously more than ready if he made a move she didn't like.

When he was within ten feet of her, he slipped from the saddle and held out the reins for Tapper, who shook his head uneasily.

Will didn't say anything, just walked forward slowly. 'It's us who helped you out of a predicament back along the trail. Besides, if I meant to do for you, ma'am, I'd have done it while you were collecting the water,' he said calmly.

'Hmm. Tell me about that *predicament*.'

Will indicated back along the trail. 'Me and my pard heard the shooting before we saw you. When you hurtled into sight we took cover. We saw the odds, thought it unreasonable and bought in. Clem there, near got his arm shot off for the satisfaction.'

The woman gave him a chary look, then she looked across to Tapper who had drawn up closer. 'He don't look too bad to me.'

Will shrugged. 'He's a tough old bird, ma'am. Then I guess the scatter-gun you're holding lets you believe what you want,' he suggested. 'So, if you don't need any more of our help, we'll just push on and forget any of this ever happened. While you're thinking on it, perhaps I'll take a look at your driver.'

The woman stepped back, watched while Will walked around to the protected, off-side of the wagon. Her eyes narrowed with anxiety as Will dragged out the near unconscious driver and propped him against a rear wheel. She was surprised by the capable, deadpan manner in which he stripped the man's shirt away from his body, stretched out his arms until the fingers of each hand clutched the spokes of the wheel. She muttered concerned curses as Will used the slim blade of his clasp knife to probe a bullet from the flesh high along the man's left shoulder, when he flinched in pain at the rough and ready surgery.

'You're lucky, it's above your collar bone,' Will told him.

'Underneath, and it would have hurt some.' He prised the driver's clenched fingers from the wheel spokes, put the bloody bullet in the man's hand and called for the woman to bring the water. 'And some clean salt,' he added.

The woman thought for a short moment, then she went to the wagon, laid the gun inside the tail flap and lifted the lid of the supplies box.

After washing the wound, Will pressed a handful of salt into the rawness. The driver's eyes exploded and he issued an agonized gasp.

'It's the squeaky wheel what gets the grease,' Will said with a wry smile. 'Seems fitting, don't you think?'

The driver took a couple of shallow breaths, looked down at the bullet and winced. 'Are you finished then?' he asked.

'Yeah,' Will said. 'Put a dressing over it,' he told the woman who was backing off. 'Then get him to town. A doctor can take care of it proper.'

After a quick reproving look towards Clem Tapper, she turned away, lifted her dress and tore off the deep fringe of her underskirt.

'You didn't say *this* had to be clean,' she said with a straight face.

Will smiled, and folded the fabric into a wad. He placed it on the wound, pulled back the man's shirt and helped him to his feet.

'You've still got the hills to get through, ma'am,' he said, turning to the woman. 'There'll be outlaws hell-bent on making or taking an easy dollar. You know what I'm saying?' Will said.

'He's right, Mrs Boe,' the driver agreed. 'It's a fair bet some o' those trails ahead are stowin' trouble. With the condition I'm in, an' with what we've got on board, I'd rather wait till tomorrow . . . at least first light.'

The woman studied the driver carefully. 'I'm not waiting,' she said and turned to face Will again. But it was Clem Tapper who spoke before she could say anything.

'Did I get that right, ma'am? He called you Mrs Boe?' he asked.

'It's my name. Constance Boe,' the woman answered back.

'Connie Boe from Alamosa?' Tapper asked, his eyes widening with interest.

'Yep, that's me. I was run out as the Righteous Brigade ran in. Have we met?'

'No ma'am, but it weren't for any goddamn virtuous beliefs. What I've heard about you an' your business fair makes my heart leap. I never figured that one day I'd get an invite.'

Connie Boe looked at Tapper sadly, took in his appearance from head to toe. 'You haven't. I doubt if you could afford the goods I've got to offer,' she said, with a curl of her upper lip.

'My name's Clemence Tapper. Clem Tapper from Denver, an' I got more'n a little baccy sack in here,' he replied unabashed, and with a squeeze of his shirt pocket. 'Yes ma'am, I got the means for one hell of a night's roosterin'. Are you thinkin' of a business in Ragland?'

'Maybe. Are you?'

Tapper beamed and turned to Will. 'This here's Connie Boe, Will. But with you bein' so young an' all, you probably walked different sides o' the street. I'm tellin' you now though, if she starts up in Ragland, I'll stand you a night that'll make you forget about pullin' out on your own. They say this lady's got enough glitter in her establishments to blind a man . . . girls so fancy, a man gets cured o' the wanderlust.'

'That's what they said in Alamosa before showing me the door, you old fool,' chided Connie Boe. She pushed Tapper out of her way and stood in front of Will. 'How do I know it was you two that stopped those outlaws from robbing us?'

Will shook his head. 'I said so, didn't I? I don't need proof.'

'I know it,' she accepted. 'I was thinking, maybe I could use you . . . your gun. I'm shipping capital . . . cash capital . . . enough for me to buy a place in Ragland.'

'Yeah? What kind o' place?' Tapper interrupted eagerly.

'A finely decorated and furnished

place with amenities for those who can afford it. A place for customers who don't want to rub shoulders with the town's drifters and riff-raff. Somewhere I can settle down, maybe. What the hell are you smiling at?' she directed at Will.

'I was wondering where these sensitive, rich patrons of yours would get their fine food and drink,' he replied. 'From what I know, Ragland doesn't provide for much more than drifters and riff-raff.'

'That means there's an opening. Why not happen along?'

'There's a couple of reasons, ma'am. For a start, your line of business ain't mine.'

'Fair enough. What else you got?'

'Not thanking us for saving your skins and your capital.' With that, Will turned away, motioned to Tapper to mount up. But Tapper didn't understand the reason for Will's brusqueness. He stayed put as Will swung on to his sorrel and lifted his hat to Connie Boe.

'Now hold on,' Connie Boe called

out. 'You're a prickly kind o' feller. Telling you I'm travelling with a pile of dollars is a lot more'n thanks in my book. Hell, most men end up thanking *me*. At least give me your name.'

'Will Stearn. Most of the time I'd fit easy with those drifters you're trying to avoid. Anyways, I'm finished here, so I'll bid you good night and be on my way.'

Will turned his horse, but before he made it back to the trail, Connie Boe fired a shot into the air.

Tapper cursed. He didn't pull his Colt, but drew back the hammer. Will turned slowly in the saddle, grinding his jaw in suppressed anger. He made no move for his own gun.

'I have to get to Ragland by morning, Mr Stearn, and I want you to ride shotgun,' the woman stated clearly. 'Your partner can trail behind and keep his eyes open. I'll pay *you* one hundred dollars and *him* fifty. That's in lieu of thanks. What do you say?'

Clem Tapper let out a quick gasp,

turned to look at Will.

'One hundred each. Me and Clem are equal partners,' Will said calmly. 'Presumably it's cash up front.'

'When we get to Ragland.'

'Looks like we're about to trust each other then.'

Connie Boe pointed to the wounded driver. 'This is Owen Hunston who's been in my employ for the last five years. I'm sure he'll establish me as a woman who's good on *that* score. I might have been thrown out of a few towns by prudes and bigots, but it was never for breaching my word.'

Will glanced at Hunston. 'Ain't that a fact,' the wounded driver agreed. 'An' no offence, but from the look o' you, you can use the money. Take time off from being a mug.'

'In addition,' pressed Connie Boe, 'you'll get a free invitation to our opening night. Best of everything on the house. Do it for your rascally old friend.'

'I've been offered a lot in my time,

ma'am, but nothing quite so *unrefusable*.' Will looked down the trail for a long moment before he slipped from the saddle and handed his reins to Tapper. 'I'm doing this for you, you old goat,' he said. 'Fix Hunston to ride the tailgate. I'll drive.'

Within a few moments, Will climbed to the driver's seat, took up the reins and waited for Connie Boe to climb aboard. He kicked off the brake, slapped the reins across the backs of the two bay mares and the wagon lurched into movement. Immediately, there was a shout of mild abuse from the bed of the wagon and Owen Hunston edged up behind the driver's bench.

'I can see you're carryin' a rind o' frost, mister, but go easy with her,' he said with a painful grin. 'She's already tamed a gunfighter husband an' a clutch o' feral towns. You so much as bruise her, an' she'll have you saddlin' a cloud.'

'Yeah? Well I'm neither of those cases,' Will replied as he worked the wagon into steady progress. Shortly, he was thinking that the extra dollars would be even more help for Clem Tapper to set up a restaurant. He also had an interesting idea about Connie Boe's clientele, wondered if the wagon could make a thousand miles to California and back, with fruit.

# 4

To Will Stearn's dust-clouded gaze, Ragland looked to be an agreeable enough town. A north-south rail link was under construction, and on the outskirts of town a sprawl of tents was already housing its track layers. Single-storey adobe and wood-frame houses of the local folk were built comfortably apart, and there was a quiet calmness about the setting. Will grinned wryly at the brick jailhouse, strangely significant at the approach to the main street. In the town proper, he noticed a diversity of stores and services that were catering for the needs of the growing population, a cattleman's bank that adjoined a double-fronted mercantile. A saloon projected showily from the boardwalk, lanes to either side, as if declaring its intention to develop. *The town's on the make. Just the place for Clem to get established*, was Will's thought. *For Connie Boe, too, if they let her.*

Will drove the wagon on through the town, noting only a casual interest afforded him by the pedestrians who mingled on both boardwalks. The fact that the interest was cursory probably meant that as a growing town, Ragland was used to strangers coming and going, if not to set down roots. He went on until he drew alongside the stage office with its purpose-built long landing, secured the brake, sat back and took a deep breath. He removed his hat and let the early warming sunlight dry out his unruly hair, remained in the driver's seat to take in the town, look for any possible premises for Clem Tapper.

'Well, I reckon we made it,' called out Connie Boe, and Will looked back to see her stepping from the wagon on to the stage platform. She appeared to be a bit wound up, but he merely shrugged and climbed down.

It took him a minute or so to work

the cramp out of his shoulders and legs, then he unhitched his horse from the back of the wagon, swung aboard and stepped up alongside her. 'Yeah, we made it, ma'am. So that'll be two hundred dollars,' he stated.

Connie Boe looked up at him, smiled with little satisfaction. 'My bags have to be off-loaded first, Mr Stearn.'

Will shook his head slowly, still not in the least annoyed by her tone or callous manner. 'Yes, ma'am. But I was hired as gun guard, not porter. If anyone ever asks me if your word's good or not, I'd like to tell them it is. Your very bond.'

Connie Boe grunted a crude epithet. She reached deep into her grip, pulled out a canvas purse and fingered some fifty dollar bills. 'The invite still goes, Mr Stearn. If I find a promising site, I can open in a week,' she said, handing Will his two hundred dollars.

'That'll be something to look forward to, ma'am, but I'm hoping to be long gone.' Will pocketed the money, nodded and turned his horse away from the platform. With Clem Tapper, he rode towards the livery stable to water and feed their mounts, settle them in for the night.

The bar room of the Bighorn Saloon was near full to capacity. The air was pungent with a mix of drink and smoke. The noise was discordant, assailed them from every direction. Will made his way to the far end of the counter where a group of cowhands made room for them. While Tapper made acquaintance, Will took a stealthy look at the gather of customers, the expected miners and ranch hands, cowboys waiting for the cattle drives to begin. There was one group of men who looked at him, but Will noticed they soon turned away when he returned the interest. He had no idea as to what they would be paying attention to, didn't think there was any reason for trouble. He decided to let the matter rest and turned back to the bar.

He was on his second beer, taking a whiskey chaser, when he noticed the tight, wiry man at his side. There was a tin star pinned to the front side of the man's battered derby, and Will gulped, almost smiled. *Like the jail . . . situated to be noticed*, was his first thought. *Son-of-a-bitch has got here quick.*

'The name's Will Stearn, lately from Colorado, Sheriff,' Will said. 'I've been in the hills working a stove-up mine with an equally stove-up partner. There's little else worth mentioning.'

'I've spoken to the driver hired by Mrs Boe. He tells me you helped swat away some ill-intentioned flies . . . says they wouldn't have made it here otherwise,' the sheriff replied. 'You don't reckon that's worth a mention?'

'Weren't much. And we were well paid for it.'

The sheriff's brow puckered. 'Are you some sort o' hired gun?' he asked, still not attempting to introduce himself.

Will shook his head. 'No, I'm not. I just told you, we're gold prospectors . . . poor ones at that.'

The sheriff took a step back for a better look. He saw Will's gun belt was a plain one, and the .36 Colt revolver, although well-fitted, was a regular model, nothing more than a drifter's companion. 'So what do you know about the Boe woman?' he asked.

Will shrugged his shoulders. He picked up the drink that was pushed his way by Tapper, who had stepped closer.

'Certainly nothing more than the driver would have told you. Anything else, you can ask *her*. It's not for me to say.'

'She's a woman who brings more'n fancy doodads as her baggage, Mr Stearn. A woman no poor gold prospector should get involved with.'

'What do you mean, involved?' Tapper put in quickly. 'Hell, can't a couple o' fellers make an easy few bucks when the chance presents itself. We don't need a pettifog lawman . . . '

'Yeah, I'll handle this, Clem,' Will said and moved to stand in Tapper's way. 'Infamous or not, Sheriff, she was

41

little more than a meal ticket for the both of us.'

The lawman sighed wearily and stood off a little more. 'I'm gettin' used to early nights, an' I'd like it to stay that way. So, you boys stay out o' trouble,' he warned, and walked away.

Will lost interest in him almost immediately. But as he contemplated another whiskey, the barkeep appeared. 'Pay him no heed,' the man offered casually. 'George Henry gets nervous if a dog barks . . . 'specially after dark.'

'Thanks, I'll remember that.' Will nodded in appreciation. He poured himself a final drink, for a while watched the barkeep go about his business. 'Get to know him, Clem,' he advised Tapper. 'He could be the one who helps you find a place to start up.'

'Why him? Apart from the obvious, how can a barkeep help me?'

'He's more than a barkeep, for chris'sakes. I'd say he was the proprietor, or close to it. And as such, all he's providing in the way of food is a jar of

42

pickled eggs. Where better to get at hungry men but during their drinking?'

'You reckon these hounds'll want to fork up a dish o' whirlups . . . sugar an' spice?'

'I don't know. You've got to start somewhere. Meantime, I'm going to take a look at the town. Is that money safe with you?'

'Yeah, how about you an' yours?'

'It's just that your eyes are running more than normal. Maybe you're thinking of the Connie Boe invitation, and want to start early,' Will said. He winked and gave Clem a friendly nudge in the chest.

As he approached the swing doors, Will saw that two of the group of men he'd noticed earlier, were coming across the room towards him. He slowed to let them go first, but they stopped, eyed him disagreeably.

'Great minds think alike, eh boys?' he offered as an appeasement.

'What do you mean?' one of the men replied sourly.

'Taking a piss. Happens to the best of us.'

The closer of the two, a short man with dark, deep-set eyes, sniffed. 'Some are more full than others,' he sneered.

Will smiled at the meaning, held their stare in silence.

'Come on, Rook. We got things to do.' The other man was just as short, but he wore a leather eye patch.

The man called Rook sucked air noisily through stained teeth, then brushed past Will on his way out through the swing doors. The other man quickly followed, a malevolent glint in his one good eye.

Outside, Will watched the two men make their way along the boardwalk. When they disappeared into the night shadows, he went to find lodgings for himself and Tapper. But he didn't want to waste time before riding from Ragland, looking for a challenge, the new opportunities.

# 5

'You impress me, Mr Stearn, but frankly, I can't say the same for your partner, Mr Tapper,' the bank manager baldly stated. 'Now, if it was *you*, I'd probably have no hesitation in arranging a loan for such a business venture . . . a restaurant.'

'So why not Clem Tapper? Have you got a reason?' Will asked.

Myles Brick was a well-informed man who oozed confidence. He was a person of the town who generally got the respect of those influenced by appearance and status. He sat forward with an unemotional smile narrowing his mouth, unsoiled hands spread across an open file.

'Like most businessmen, I'm au fait with what's going on in Ragland, Mr Stearn,' he started. 'As for our banking system, it's best to know about someone who intends to make use of it. The same way in which you would look at a horse's feet before buying it, I suppose.'

'There's a big difference,' Will replied with quick, marked coolness. 'I asked you for the *reason*.'

The manager looked irritated and got to his feet, stood behind the desk for his height to make an impression. 'This wasn't meant to get personal, Mr Stearn, but, when a thousand dollars of this bank's money is involved, I do have the right . . . '

'I'm not doubting that. Just get to the point about Clem Tapper. What do you know?' Will interceded.

'He's a trouble-maker.'

'When? Where?'

'Brawling in the Bighorn. He was involved on both occasions.'

'That's ridiculous,' Will protested. 'If you only made loans to those who weren't involved in some sort of brawling, you'd have the fattest safe inside and outside of Christendom.

Besides, the sheriff said he didn't have anything to answer for.'

'That's as maybe. But the fact is, he was in the thick of it. What we look for when making a substantial loan is standing and stability. It's about references, Mr Stearn, and all I'm hearing so far is trouble.'

'There'll always be trouble in growing towns . . . towns like this, for chris'sakes,' Will continued. 'Where do you think you've set up business, heaven's high city?'

'Steady, Mr Stearn, I didn't say I wouldn't make the loan. I'm just not that impressed, so far. I'd like to see if the prospective investment calms down. Come and see me again in one week . . . one trouble-free week. Ragland *is* growing like you say, and I'm all for encouraging new and exciting ventures. What do you say?'

'I'd say a week's one hell of a long time. And your little town's far too full of trouble.'

'Touché,' Brick smiled resignedly.

'But let's just see if Mr Tapper can overcome the ordeal. Within a few months the rail link gets here. So staying out of trouble will be worth it. And now, if you don't mind, I'm a busy man, Mr Stearn.'

Will rose and turned to leave. 'Yeah, I thought I was too,' he muttered in reply. 'Let's just call it a day.' Without a backward glance he went out, closing the door carefully behind him. Alone, outside the office, he cursed his old friend. He didn't want to waste any more time, and now he'd been given the ultimatum of a whole week. He cursed again, left the bank and crossed the street to the Bighorn Saloon.

Clem Tapper was at the counter, holding forth with a group of cowhands. He was already well on the way to being drunk, even though it was still early afternoon. His voice was slurred, and to Will it seemed to fill the room.

Tapper turned quickly around when, in the back-bar mirror, he saw Will approaching. Guilt showed in his eyes, and his jaw and shoulders dropped in accord.

'Finish your drink and come back to the lodgings, Clem. There's something we've got to talk about,' Will said.

Tapper swayed, then took a small, backwards and sideways step. 'What for, Will? You said I was to rub shoulders, establish myself.'

'Take him with you, mister, or I'll throw him out myself,' a harsh voice cut across the room. 'He's got my ears that sore with his guff.'

Will turned to meet the man's threat. He recognized him immediately as the short man called Rook who had shown disdain for him on their first night in town. He had seen him since back in the saloon, apparently filling time at the card tables. He was in the company of a big man called Hoke Plantin. On one occasion they had been joined by two other men, as memorably unprepossessing and malevolent looking as themselves.

Will motioned Tapper to walk away.

But Tapper nodded towards Plantin and Rook. 'They never give up, Will,' he growled. 'Every goddamned time I've set foot in the place, they start. Last night they had a real go after you'd gone.'

Will took a deep breath. He was thinking of all the other scraps that Clem Tapper had created, when he saw the sneer working its way across Plantin's face. He indicated again that Tapper should leave. 'It's best we go,' he said.

Then, as he guessed he would, Plantin pushed. 'Yeah, get the ol' bore out o' here. An' keep him out,' his voice blasted.

All of a sudden the silence in the bar room was palpable. The saloonist, Felix June, who had shown some affability towards Tapper since they had arrived in town, wiped a cloth through the beer puddles as he edged slowly along the counter.

'Watch it, mister,' he muttered. 'Like coyotes, they work together to pull their prey down.'

Focused on the street doors, Will pushed Tapper forward. But he had only walked a few paces, when Plantin called out again.

'An' stay to hell out o' here yourself. My liquor don't go down so well in front of either o' you turkeys.'

'Meet me back at the room . . . my room,' Will told Tapper.

'The hell I will. If there's goin' to be trouble, I'm in, you know it.'

'If there's trouble and you're any-where near it, you don't get your restaurant. I'll sort this out. Wait by the doors for me.' Will turned away and walked back towards the bar. He stopped at the card table, looked calmly down on the players.

Plantin looked big sitting in his chair, sneering now, his face crumpling with grim expectation. His muscled forearms were resting on the table, huge fists bunching. 'What are *you* comin' back for?' he asked.

'You've hurt my friend's feelings, big feller,' Will said. 'Now, if you were to get up and tell him sorry . . . that you made a mistake, he might just forgive and forget. Of course, you'd still have *me* to answer to.'

Rook swore and tried to get to his feet, but Will's hand reached out and shoved him down again. 'Stay put,' he rasped. 'This is between me and the ugly great pig sitting here next to you. If he wants to fight, let him have the chance.'

Will's manner was calm, but there was a tenseness in him which Plantin immediately recognized and didn't like. The man came to his feet. He rolled his huge body upright with an indolence meant to tell the whole room that he could handle not only Will, but anybody else who wanted in.

Will moved off, his back to him, and Plantin followed slowly out to the street. After a few moments a body of eager customers jostled through the doors to witness the confrontation.

Felix June came hurriedly from behind his counter, waved Clem Tanner across when he saw Rook pushing his way through the spectators. 'Your man looks like he can handle himself. Can he?' he asked.

Tanner looked anxiously about him. 'Yeah, he can take him. Two of 'em might be a problem. 'Specially if they came in by surprise.'

'It'll only be one. Trust me,' June said. He reached back over the counter, searched for a big .44 Army Colt. He pushed the gun into his belt, drew his waistcoat across to conceal it and stepped out to the boardwalk.

Hoke Plantin was standing in the afternoon's sunlight. He was rolling up his sleeves and Will was waiting for him, his face expressionless.

Plantin looked scornfully around him, then lumbered forward. Will appeared relaxed, remained unmoved when Plantin swung a heavy fist at his head. He went under the blow, pounded a weighty left into Plantin's stomach. The blow lifted Plantin on to his toes, then a bone-cracking right ripped at the point of his jaw.

A gasp went up from some of the crowd. 'He'll break his hand, you see,' Clem Tapper said with quiet, sober concern. 'What good'll he be then?'

Will moved more quickly now. He crowded in, both hands moving like pistons, his punches smacking at Plantin's face. The big man was losing ground and he twisted himself into the narrow side lane. He stumbled against a high fence, recoiled in anger and bowled out a defensive fist. But Will side-stepped, clipped a hard, accurate blow between Plantin's darkening eyes.

Plantin's hands dropped, and he stood immobile. His mouth sagged open and he stared ahead blankly, unsure of who or where he was.

Will reached out and grabbed the front of the man's coat, swung him around and booted him back into the fence. Plantin crumpled, and Will wiped his hands down his sides, flexed the painful bones of his fingers.

'Stay there, goddamnit. You're down

with your friends,' he said.

Not far off a run, Sheriff Henry was advancing down the street. He stopped, shook his head when he saw Will emerge from the lane.

'Goddamnit it, Stearn, I should've known. Where the hell's Tapper?' he demanded.

'It wasn't anything to do with him, Sheriff. And there was no gun play. It was two men, settling something the only way one of them knew how,' Will assured him.

'I won't tell you again, Clem,' he added, knowing Tapper was watching close by, within earshot. 'Keep your mouth shut and move.'

# 6

In the Bighorn Saloon that night, a few of the drinking men were talking about Hoke Plantin paying a visit to the town doctor. Those who had waited on the outcome, said that when he came out, his face was mottled with bruising, his mouth and jaw were swollen and a lot of his usual swagger was gone.

Standing alone at the bar, Will Stearn was mulling over his own circumstances. Even if he hadn't been coerced by Myles Brick to stay in Ragland for another week, he would have done. It wasn't in his nature to ride away from a threat. He knew he would have to go up against Plantin sometime. And better to be around, than to let old Clem suffer the outcome.

Will was contemplating the food situation, or the lack of it, when Sheriff George Henry sent him word for a meeting at the jailhouse. But the messenger had hardly left the bar, when Felix June approached him.

'I've got somethin' to tell you,' he said, leaning closer. 'It's no secret, more like undisclosed, until things are . . . '

'Until things are what?' Will asked impatiently.

'More settled. I'm probably goin' into business with Clem. I've got the two side rooms we can get organized . . . put a stove in one of 'em. I've got enough tables an' chairs an' spare pots an' plates. Ain't got nothin' to cook, o' course, but Clem says that's his side o' the partnership. Between us there's no reason we can't get goin' right away. There'll be no need for you to try an' wring money out of a goddamn bank.'

Will studied him intently, surprised and unsure of the man's motive. Experience had taught him that one man rarely helped another without good reason. He was also unhappy about June knowing his business at the bank. But that wouldn't really be June's fault.

'Sounds interesting,' he opened tentatively. 'But you'll have to chew it finer.'

June could see the thought, the hint of doubt. 'Back seven years, I was driftin' with a few owly friends down Mexico way,' he said. 'None of us had any real interest in anythin', but then I met this lonely wife of some rich hidalgo. I reckon she helped me for no other damned reason than she liked what she saw. It certainly weren't my brains she was after. She had a line o' cantinas along the border, an' gave me one, sayin' I'd never thank her. Anyways, she was wrong. I made it pay good, an' she let me sell out for a fair profit. Since then, I've worked places, bigger places, but now I'm settled at Bighorn. With Clem's help I reckon we can make a lot more business.'

Will continued thinking while June poured them a drink. 'So there's no reason for you to stay on, not if you don't want. Clem reckons you've lifted the trouble off him, but landed it on yourself. You've put yourself in danger, an' Newton Boe is on the way to Ragland. He might even be here now.'

'Boe? A relation of Connie Boe?'

'Husband. Do you know him?'

Will shook his head, but thought he'd been referred to him indirectly. He leant further across the counter to catch more information.

'He's a gunman with a reputation as long as this bar. Him an' his wife haven't been on speakin' terms for some time, but some say she'll take him back once she gets her place up an' runnin'. She'll need someone.'

Will sipped his drink. It was all a bit soon, and he couldn't square his own plans, or why Felix June should be concerned about his safety.

'Hoke Plantin's one of his sidekicks. An' so's Rook,' June went on.

'He's not too big on style then, this Boe feller?'

'Huh? Well, yeah, as I was sayin'. Owen Hunston, who drove Mrs Boe here, is somewhere centre in terms o' loyalty. But that don't mean he gets to buck ol' Newton.'

Will frowned, pushed his glass forward for a refill. 'What's this to do with me? What exactly are you drivin' at?'

'I'm goin' into business with Clem. Between us we can handle Plantin, but not with you around. Believe me, mister, I didn't arrive here in Ragland by walkin' away from trouble. Right now I'm at the end of a long chain o' circumstances an' keen to get that eatery established. With Clem Tapper arrivin', I've got the chance, the opportunity. We haven't quite come to terms yet, so maybe that's why you don't know the detail. But the deal won't work if you stay. I'm not havin' any truck with Newton Boe.'

Now, Will more understood June, and with a half-smile, drained his glass. From the street came the strains of music and shouting, and he shook his head, held the flat of his hand out at the offer of yet another shot of whiskey.

Like everybody else in the bar, he turned to search out the cause of the high spirits.

'Sign's not up yet, but it's the openin' of the Rojo Pluma. It's at the end of the street,' June explained. 'She's true to her word . . . didn't waste any time gettin' things started.'

'No,' Will said, as though he had something else on his mind. He was thinking that with Clem set up comfortably, from now on nothing much in the town should interest him. He could be gone by morning, and to hell with Plantin and his friends. 'Where is Clem?' he asked.

'Last I seen of him he was goin' to look for you. He certainly won't be asleep, not with *that* noise.'

'Hey fellers, it's the girls . . . all packed aboard a genuine cat wagon,' a customer shouted as Will pushed his way through. Will got to the swing doors in time to see a brightly-painted, concord coach trundling slowly along the street. Connie Boe was dressed in a scarlet costume of silk and feathers, and rode beside Owen Hunston. From the windows, a bevy of young women smiled gleefully, waved ribbons and garters.

Connie Boe looked up as Will stepped out to the edge of the boardwalk. 'Fresh in from Silver City, Mr Stearn. It's going to be a real grand opening, and your invitation stands. Come on down and see the fun,' she called out.

Will heard a low harrumphing beside him, turned to see the sheriff frowning at the coach and the small, bawdy cavalcade that followed. Will was aware of the snooty undercurrent against Connie Boe. The more straitlaced citizens wanted her run from town before she had a chance to corrupt the minds and morals of the younger generation. Whether their sentiments were enough to combat the eagerness of others was very doubtful. 'I hope they let us in . . . just wish I was a few years younger,' seemed to be the general consensus of men at the bar.

'Pa, are you really going to let this happen?' the question came.

Attracted by the incongruity of the voice, Will found himself looking at a woman as good-looking as any he'd seen in a long time. She was in her early twenties, slim and modestly dressed. Her long raven hair was pulled back, showed her features to be a little sharper than her father's.

As sheriff, George Henry was always going to be caught up in the town's predicament no matter what he personally thought. 'What the hell can I do, girl? She's broken no laws that I know of,' he said. 'Besides . . . '

'Yes, *besides*. *Besides* you don't mind. The town's supposed to be getting civilized, Pa. There's ordinance you uphold concerning breaches of the peace and public places.'

'Keep out of this, Rose. If her or hers starts to make trouble, I'll close 'em down. I was going to say there's quite a few accountable folk in this town who regard Connie Boe as a provider of entertainment. She's given me her assurance that Rojo Pluma will be run properly. There's not going to be any dubious sign above the door, as them temperance society bygones seem to think.'

Rose Henry glared at her father. She would have gone on arguing if she hadn't suddenly noticed Will Stearn looking at her. His interest was so open it made her flush with embarrassment.

Henry saw the look, but was reassured to find the cause was somebody he knew. 'What do you think, Mr Stearn?' he enquired. 'Do you think the morals of this town are about to get compromised?'

'My thinking doesn't come into it, Sheriff. But I'd have thought the Rojo Pluma — or whatever it's going to be called — is entitled to at least one crack of the whip, so to speak. Why don't you wait and see?' While Will spoke, he held Rose's look as though being more interested in *her* response.

'I'm goin' to. I know it's bein' run on invitation only, an' there's not goin' to be any drunks fallin' in from the boardwalk. Those girls are like hostesses apparently, with a percentage o' the take. It's up to the customers how much they spend. I can't see what's wrong with that. It's how most o' the other town merchants do business.'

'Yeah, quite so, Sheriff. Through professional courtesy, I have my own invite, but I'd have gone anyway, if I had the money,' Will said and grinned easily.

Rose snorted and stepped past her father. 'Well, that's very convenient, Mr Stearn. From what I've heard, it's saving that woman's money from robbers that's got you the invitation. The notoriety of your street fighting and getting drunk, must have helped. What else are you going to do, other than make sounds of approval. Nevertheless, I'll ask you kindly not to encourage my father in this . . . this barefaced vulgarity.'

Will looked thrown. 'You got me wrong, ma'am,' he started. 'I like a drink, sure, but the fighting was mainly on someone else's behalf. Besides, the lane was a dark, rank old place and not so much one for the general public. As for your father, well, a town sheriff's supposed to think and speak for himself.'

Henry opened his mouth to protest or join in, but Will was ready to continue.

'There's never enough women to go around in emergent, frontier towns. Most of the men who've fetched up in Ragland aren't going to be unaffected by the charm of a pretty woman. I'm neither for Mrs Boe's establishment nor against it, ma'am. In fact, I'm not for or against *anything* in this town. I'm about to head west . . . or north.'

Now the sheriff did speak. He was interested, and ignored the response his daughter was about to make. 'Soon?' he asked.

'As soon as I can find Clem Tapper.

There's one or two little matters about our partnership that need to be settled.'

'I'm not restin' much easier.'

'That's your problem, Sheriff. I'm certainly not making it mine,' Will retorted. Then he touched the brim of his hat to Rose and walked off.

As he walked slowly down the boardwalk he nodded to Myles Brick, who was talking animatedly to another well-dressed townsman. From the men's body language, it was obvious to Will that they weren't unhappy with the arrival of Connie Boe and her Rojo Pluma. From what he overheard on passing, Ragland's prospering men wanted to spend their money on something more lavish than what was currently on offer.

With mixed thoughts, Will turned towards the end of town. He checked on the feed and stabling for his sorrel, that it would be in near readiness for his departure. He went back to the main street to continue looking for Tapper, walking on until he mingled with the gathering outside of Rojo Pluma.

He could see in through the open doorway of the premises, was surprised that a lot of the interior refurbishments had got stacked on the bed of a single mud wagon.

He stood enjoying the presence of the crowd, the lively comments that, unsurprisingly, ran counter to Rose Henry's. He absorbed the company and friendly atmosphere, at the same time suffering a trace of regret at the trail ahead.

A few minutes later, he was turning into the lodgings when he saw Clem Tapper on the opposite boardwalk. Tapper was staggering along, staring ahead, and Will watched him approach the Rojo Pluma. Will cursed softly when Tapper exchanged a word with one of two men who were minding the doorway, more forcefully when he went in.

The doorkeepers were inspecting the invitations which Connie Boe had freely handed about the town. The tickets were supposedly for prominent businessmen, but Will was let through with an informed nod.

The decoration of the room disguised its crude structure. A brightly-lit interior boasted three crystal chandeliers and a curved bar with velvet plush stools fronting it. In the far corner was an upright piano and a stage with red drapes. It wasn't much smaller than the Bighorn saloon, but there the comparison ended. Connie Boe was presenting an ornamental splendour that Rose Henry and the town's bigots couldn't disregard, only disapprove of.

Will was handed a complimentary drink by one of the welcome girls, and then he mingled with the openly admiring guests. Connie saw him and, breaking away from a pair of potential customers, sashayed her way across.

'Your thoughts?' she asked him.

'Looks real fine, ma'am. Can't fail.' Taking the opportunity to look around, Will was wondering where Clem Tapper was.

'I've just been told that within a month, I'll have the whole town eating out of my hand.'

Will smiled at the turn of phrase, thought that Clem and Felix June might have something to say about that.

'I'll run clean card games,' she continued. 'My roulette wheel will be honestly operated, and all my girls will answer to me. The customers will be tripping over each other to get in. Why don't you stay and watch me get rich . . . *help* me get rich?'

'It's not what I do, ma'am. I prefer trail dust,' Will said.

'Yeah, you would. Just remember it clogs the works.' Connie Boe accepted Will's reply with a warm smile, then after raising her glass as a farewell gesture, she went back to work her guests.

Will hadn't wished her good luck, but it was a promising start. He was thinking that by the time he did come back, she might be a good friend to have. *Probably be goddamn mayor*, he thought. He wandered around the place, but couldn't see any sign of Clem Tapper. Relieved but puzzled, he exited by a screened side door and turned towards the front street. 'He must've come this way,' he muttered, closing the door against the clamour of appreciation for Rojo Pluma's delights.

He stopped a few paces short of the main street, a sixth sense warning him of trouble. He shuddered and turned sharply, looking back into the ominous shadows. From beyond the door he had just come out of, he heard a cough, then a groan of pain. 'Clem,' he called. 'Clem, are you there?'

A moment later Clem Tapper stumbled forward. He carried the sickening filth of the side lane across his body, and his grimy hands were outstretched and groping. Even in the failing light Will could see the streaks of dark blood across his face. Then Tapper pitched forward, turning away as though in shame.

# 7

Will dragged Tapper into a sitting position, propped him up against the building's timber sleepers.

'Christ, you're meant to be writing up fancy bills of fare, not taking a beating,' he muttered. When his old friend stirred, blinked his eyes, Will used his thumb to wipe away a gobbet of blood from his swollen cracked lips. 'Why'd this happen, Clem? Who the hell did it?' he asked.

Tapper swallowed, clutched hard at Will's wrist. 'It's that woman, Will. Connie Boe,' he rasped. 'She's as crooked as a snake in a cactus patch. I've lost everythin' . . . every straw cent.'

'How? There wasn't any gambling that I could see.'

'It's a card game, in one o' the back rooms, behind a big red curtain. That husband o' hers is there, an' Plantin. They cleaned me out real quick. I bucked 'em, said I wanted to see Mrs Red Feathers herself . . . the big augur. Reckon that's why they beat me up.'

Will helped Tapper to his feet. 'You've taken worse than this, Clem. You're not about to die on me,' he said, encouragingly. 'Breathe shallow, it don't hurt so much. This time you go back to the rooms. Go straight back and don't drink anything. It'll make you cough. Just wait for me.'

Tapper took a step sideways, grunted and shook his head in despair. 'Yeah, OK. I've done it again, haven't I? Make a mess for you to come along an' clear up.'

'Just stay there until I come back.'

'There's a handful of 'em, Will. An' that Boe feller, he's a snake. A real mean one. Don't even look him in the eye.'

'That might be difficult,' Will answered back. He took hold of Tapper's shoulder and guided him back out of the lane towards the main street. 'Stay in the open. You'll be safe enough, and I'll see you soon,' he said.

Will watched Tapper for a moment, then he returned to the lane, back to the side entrance of the Rojo Pluma. He turned the door handle, but now it was locked.

'Take more than that to keep me out, you sons-of-bitches,' he snorted angrily. He set himself back a step and rammed the heel of his boot at a low point of the door. The timber gave, the door smashed inwards and Will stepped quickly into the brightly lit interior.

Hoke Plantin and Owen Hunston who had been standing near, heard the crash, turned and saw Will. Brushing the curtain screen aside, they moved quickly, Plantin dropping a hand for his Colt. But Will was more than ready. He reached out and grabbed the man's wrist, and spun him hard against the inner wall.

Hunston cursed and made a lunge for Will.

'Get back,' Will rasped at him. 'I'll

break your friend's neck if you try anything stupid. I'm getting real pep-pery at you people.'

'What the hell do you want, Stearn?'

'Connie Boe. Tell her I want to see her right away or I burn this place down with everyone in it. Those grand, hanging lanterns will be lighting the place from the floor up.'

Hunston backed off and Plantin tried to wrest himself free. Will slammed him back against the wall, crushing his pulpy nose. Plantin spluttered in pain, his shoulders sagged and Will let him go, watching as the big man crumpled to the floor. He stood glowering, glaring down on the gunman. 'Seems you can't get enough of me hammering your great ugly mug.' Will was now filling with resentment, in dangerous mood if the provocation and harm continued.

Hunston came back a few moments later, shaking his head. 'She's not around. Not that I could see anyway. Could be she's with the girls, gettin' 'em painted for tonight's show. An' that ain't somethin' I'd want to intrude on, mister.'

'Where's the card game?' Will snapped.

A look of sly surprise came over Hunston's face and he shook his head again. 'There's no game here tonight. The lady figures on lettin' her customers get the feel o' the place. It's tomorrow that she starts business, proper.'

'There's a game and you know it,' Will said sharply. 'It's the game that Clem Tapper lost his stake in. Now show me where it is, or I will do to you what you did to him.'

Hunston backed off. He looked about him sheepishly, was considering his options when a store-room door to his right opened. Two men who were arguing fervently were being pushed out. They saw Will, and one of them turned on him, angrily.

'You in on stealin' from us, are you, Stearn? You in with these slimy card-sharps?'

'Watch your mouth feller.' There was a snarl from inside the room and the man known as Rook came out to prod the two townsmen forward. When he too saw Will he moved his hand defensively towards his Colt.

'What the hell's goin' on? What are *you* doin' here?' he demanded.

'I'm looking for Mr or Mrs Boe.'

'He's in here,' Rook said, indicating with a nod over his shoulder. 'Game's folded a tad earlier than expected.'

But Hoke Plantin was back on his feet. He was cupping a big hand around the meat of his bloody nose, glaring malevolently.

'Leave him be, Stearn,' Rook advised Will. 'You done him enough damage.'

'Yeah, why don't you try someone different?' Hunston said. He looked around him quickly, as though checking it was OK to fight, then came in with his fists bunched.

Will shifted back a step, catching a blow on his forearm. He steadied himself and drove a very quick punch through Hunston's fists and into his stomach. Hunston gasped and folded over and Will moved forward into him.

'I like this close stuff,' he grated, 'and you shouldn't have lied about the card game.' He was about to force a short hard finisher up to Hunston's jaw, when he caught a glimpse of a dark shape swinging towards him from the doorway. He ducked, only had time to curse and think he'd spoken too soon, before a gun barrel cracked into the side of his head. He felt his body slump and his legs go numb, but he stopped himself from going down.

'Hold him up.' The voice was harsh and full of authority.

Will felt two sets of hands grip him. He tried to shrug himself free, blink some clear sight, but all he saw was the blurred features of Owen Hunston. Then he gasped in pain when the man's fist pounded into his ribs.

As though through sodden, water-filled ears, Will heard the voice again.

'You've both had your chance, now stand back. Find yourselves some other work.'

Will lifted his head. A spare, dark-suited figure stood directly in front of him. The man had a face from which all colour had drained, and his high cheekbones were taut against his skin. His unflickering eyes were grey and cruel.

'This is my warning to you, Stearn,' Newton Boe growled. 'What goes on here's our business, so stay out of it. I don't want to see you anywhere near this place again. Preferably *anywhere* again.'

'You and me think the same, mister,' Will managed. 'Only trouble is, your circle of bugs and runts keep giving me reason to stay.'

By way of an answer, Boe packed the frame of his Colt against the side of Will's head. Will was expecting such a retaliation and he rode some of the blow. But pain exploded through his skull, spread to blunt, thumping hurt as blows landed across his neck and shoulders. He could hear the heavy breathing as Boe laid into the beating and as he went down, he gave a rueful smile at the irony of Newton Boe being a renowned gunman. Then there was nothing but blackness, no more thoughts or feelings.

*　*　*

He smelled the perfume first, sickly sweet as it fused with the odour of his own blood. Will opened his eyes slowly, but immediately the hurt swept through him. Nearly every inch of his body ached. He blinked a couple of times to clear his vision, looked at the hazy outline of Connie Boe.

'Looks like you met Gorgon,' she said. 'I was told you'd been beaten badly, that you wanted to see me.'

'Yeah, that was before I got pistol-whipped,' Will replied.

'I don't hold with that sort of treatment, Mr Stearn. Not for anyone,' Connie Boe retaliated with what looked and sounded like genuine surprise. 'I'm certainly not to blame . . . no matter what.'

'Not to blame?' Will echoed incredulously. 'It's your goddamn establishment that Clem Tapper was playing his cards in. He told me he was cheated, and I went in to check it out. Your husband and two or three of his pack took exception.'

The light from the side doorway of Rojo Pluma showed Connie Boe's aggrieved expression. 'Newton did this?' she asked.

'Yeah, Gorgon. Your husband. He fits the description. Now if you don't mind, I'd like to get the hell out of here.'

Connie Boe nodded, but stood her ground, watched Will with close interest. 'Regardless of what you've been told, there was no card game tonight, Mr Stearn,' she said. 'Tapper must have imagined it, through drink perhaps. As for the beating you've taken, well, you must have really pushed Newton. He's a mean son-of-a-bitch at the best of times. But if you've got reckoning on your mind, I suggest you calm down. Leave it to me. How much is Tapper supposed to have lost?'

'Everything. Close to three hundred fifty dollars. He must have spent some . . . say three hundred even.'

'Hmm. Wait outside. Not in here. I'll be back shortly.'

Will knew there was nothing broken, but his mouth was dried out and he felt sore all over his body. What 'lifers' in Yuma called beatin' the sap out of. He held little fear for Newton Boe, but his blood was running hot. His frame of mind was encouraging a gunfight, but he knew he wouldn't be winning it.

Connie Boe waited until Will was into the gloom of the lane before she went inside. When she came out again, Will was contemplating the blood stains across the front of his shirt.

'Tell whoever washes it not to use hot water,' she offered, handing him a bundle of notes. 'I can't find Newton. But then he's not supposed to be here,' she continued. 'And I can't understand how he managed to organize a card game right under my nose. Still, here's Tapper's money with an extra fifty for his trouble. Take it and stay well away from that husband of mine. He'll kill you.'

'Yeah, he told me as much.' Will attempted a careless smile. He was considering brushing her aside, when angry shouting came from the main street, a threatening bellow from George Henry.

'Goddamnit, that's all I need,' Connie Boe cried out. She threw a weary look at Will. 'I wonder what Bolivia's like?' she said, before hurrying to find out the cause of the latest trouble.

# 8

The Rojo Pluma was almost deserted. Owen Hunston took one look at Will before leaving through the front doors. Will followed him to the tumult of noise outside.

On the boardwalk, George Henry was shoving two men to the main street. 'I'll take care o' this, Dubble,' he was saying. 'Get back an' don't cause trouble.'

Will recognized the two men who had emerged arguing out of the card room at the point of Rook's gun. Jed Callow was the taller, more significant looking, the most voluble.

'You want to know what happened, Sheriff? Well I'll tell you. Me an' Dubb were robbed. It ain't the losin' for chris'sakes . . . hell I've done that most o' my life. No, it's bein' cheated. This establishment is bad and if *you* don't

84

close it . . . *we will*.'

'You'll do no such thing, Jed. That's for the law.'

Newton Boe stepped from the edge of the interested, gathering crowd, stood where most could see him. His hard bearing silenced both Dubble and Callow instantly.

George Henry turned to see what was going on. 'You're Boe. Newton Boe,' he stated gruffly.

'Yeah,' the gunman agreed. 'That mean something to you, Sheriff?'

'If this isn't your business, stay out. If it is, keep quiet until I've considered this man's complaint . . . in full. *That's* what it means,' Henry rasped back.

'You're listenin to the gripe of a bad loser. His luck ran foul, an' all you're doin' is lettin' him bad mouth me in public. There's a law against that. So, you clear this crowd away from here, before I forget my social graces.'

Henry coloured a little, but stood his ground. 'I'm the *law* here Boe, an' you best remember it,' he snapped. 'These

85

men claim to have been cheated an' they're goin' to have their say. Now shut up before my old sworn-in Colt forgets *its* goddamn social graces.'

Boe sniffed thoughtfully and the rest of the crowd began to withdraw a little. All except Rose who walked straight up to stand beside her father and smile reassuringly.

'Your kind aren't wanted in this town,' she said, with a scornful glare at Boe. 'This is a peaceful community, intent on minding its own civil business. At least trying to. So why don't you pack up and get out. And take your wife with you.'

Boe glowered back at her. Will thought a touch of admiration crossed his rough face, and he almost smiled.

But before Boe could respond, his wife pushed forward from the side lane. Men stepped aside until she too gained a place to be heard alongside the sheriff.

'If any of you men have a grievance, I'll listen and check the matter out personally,' she said loudly. 'If any of you have been cheated, you'll be compensated. I didn't approve or know of any illegitimate gambling tonight, and that goes for the future. I promised you I'd run a clean house, and as long as I'm able I will.'

Connie Boe's words rolled over the heads of the crowd. Jed Callow broke the silence by continuing with his accusation.

'In less than fifteen minutes, I lost a hundred an' fifty dollars in one o' your back rooms. You might not have known about it, ma'am, but it happened. It's not what you'd call a *clean* house.'

Connie Boe stared back for a long moment. 'Fair enough, mister. I'm sorry but I'll stand by what I said. If any of you have been taken by a rigged game, I'll make good. Now, has anybody else got something to say while we're at it?'

There was a brooding silence in the street, and George Henry was ill at ease because his authority had been usurped. He led his daughter across to a small group of businessmen who were talking with Connie Boe.

'Well handled, ma'am. But Jed Callow had more than a fair point, an' I'm closin' your place until his accusation's been checked out,' he said. 'You don't open until *I* say you can.'

Now Newton Boe shifted forward again, but with a degree of caution. Hoke Plantin was close to him and on the edge of the boardwalk. Rook was standing idly behind Plantin, against an overhang support.

'You can't close anybody down, Sheriff,' Boe growled. 'The Rojo Pluma stays open. Anybody wantin' action can come in an' get it any time.'

Rose stared anxiously at her father, who merely pointed down the boardwalk, each way in turn.

Newton Boe looked, saw at least three men spread out around them. They were partly in the shadows off the main street, but it was plain they carried shot-guns to cover him, Plantin and Rook.

'I know of your reputation with a gun, Mr Boe,' Henry said calmly. 'But when you're hit with a few ounces o' buckshot, you'll be slowed down some.'

'They only want an excuse, boss,' Plantin said nervously.

Boe went on looking until he had summed up the position. 'You got the deadwood, Sheriff . . . for now. It won't always be like this.'

'It will be as long as I'm wearin' this badge. This might not be the most prime town you've ever passed through, but there's a few folk here who've met your kind before, Mr Boe. They'll stand up to you. Your friend, Mr Plantin's, already noticed. He's smarter than he looks.'

From the doorway of the Rojo Pluma, Will was watching closely, could see that Newton Boe was making a decision. The man was wondering whether to trust in the ability of Rook and Plantin, or to climb down. A nerve twitched in his face.

But, mindful of the interest in her words, Connie Boe decided it was time to continue her pitch. She faced George Henry.

'If you want to delay the opening, Sheriff, that's how it'll be,' she said. 'I own this place and I'll run it according to whatever bylaws you and the town decide. You're welcome to visit me any time and test my games of chance. In fact, you can use my dollars to do it. But please don't leave it too long. Time really is money in this business.'

'What about *my* money, Mrs Boe?'

Connie Boe turned her attention to Jed Callow. 'Put in your claim,' she said. 'Now I've got an early closing to attend to,' she added to no one in particular.

When her husband went to follow her, she swung furiously on him. 'That was your biggest mistake, Newt,' she seethed. 'We're through, and I don't want to see your face again. I mean it. And don't come looking for handouts or try to rob me again. Hell, I knew it was you up on the ridge. You and your pariah dogs.'

Taken aback, Boe cursed, stopped mid-stride and returned her steely glare. Equally surprised, Plantin and Rook backed slowly up against the wall of the building. They were still conscious of the threat of the guns levelled on them.

Henry, trying to keep his daughter from getting involved, saw Will moving slowly through the crowd. Will's bruised face and grim expression told him all he needed to know and he quickly stepped forward. 'Hold it, Stearn, I know what you're thinkin',' he advised. 'I heard what happened to Tapper,' he continued when Will turned to face him. 'Seems you too ran into more trouble than you could handle. But that's where it ends. No gunplay.'

Boe heard the lawman's warning. He looked at Will and spat on the boardwalk. Then he shot a quick hard look at his wife, motioned Plantin and Rook to accompany him down the street.

'Just let 'em go,' Henry said. 'Best thing for you to do is get the hell out o' Ragland before I have to order your box.'

*You're the second one to suggest that*, Will thought, as Henry persisted.

'No one's doubting the fact that you're capable or that you've got guts, Stearn. I've got some o' them myself. But I've also got help against that sort. What I've heard about Newton Boe makes me jumpy. Seems he pushes men into a gunfight, just like he's pushin' you. Goddamnit, he's headed for the Territory's 'most wanted' list.'

Will looked at Rose Henry. He could see she was appalled by the state he was in, the cuts and bruises on his face. He felt that her opinion of him wasn't getting any better.

'Best let the doc have a look at you, before you ride,' Henry advised.

'That's thoughtful of you. Where?'

'I'm talkin' about Doc Weaver. He's first house down on the right beyond the jailhouse. He'll take care o' you, the same way I'm takin' care o' the town.'

Will levelled an unfriendly look at the sheriff, then without another word went off down the boardwalk towards the Bighorn Saloon. He heard Henry's curse, winced at the ache in his arm as he drew his Colt, gave a needless checking glance at the fully loaded chamber.

He was approaching the saloon when Clem Tapper suddenly appeared ahead of him.

'Yeah, don't move from the room, I know,' Tapper said, stopping within figurative slapping range. 'But I was hurtin' Will . . . needed some physic. That's OK surely?'

'Of course it is, Clem. I'm sorry, I should've thought. A half bottle of Felix June's stagger soup for what ails you, eh? Hah, I'm treading the same path.'

'Yeah, but listen Will. June says there's three of 'em layin' for you, bringin' down a real whiskey war dance. Even with me tagged along, you've got no chance.'

'I'll make one, Clem. I always have.'

'Not this time, Will. Tonight's wrong. Boe's already been wound-up by the sheriff, an' he's meaner'n a stuck boar. Besides, you're in no condition to fight him . . . *them*. You've been dead-armed

. . . probably in a few other places . . . that's what the beatin' was.'

Will took a deep, steadying breath. 'Yeah. I guess the son-of-a-bitch knew what he was doing,' he rasped.

'Workin' on his advantage. Right now, you'd be slower'n a sick mule.'

Will studied his old friend intently for a moment, then nodded in agreement. 'OK, Clem. Perhaps a night's rest will make it all go away.' As he turned towards the lodgings, he saw that George Henry had followed him from the Rojo Pluma, was openly watching him as he headed for his room.

# 9

For the next three days, every person in Ragland capable of stringing a few words together had something to say about Connie Boe and her infamous husband. The continuing presence of Will Stearn was also a cause for concern. It was obvious the man was waiting for something, but only George Henry knew what. He had seen Will talking to Clem Tapper, the resigned body language, had guessed the significance. He knew that Will wanted Newton Boe, would be making his move as soon as it was viable.

At first, Rose Henry had taken exception to Will and his rough conduct. But she had been much influenced by her father, had a careful regard for men who could stand on their own two feet. Being witness to any kind of violence genuinely sickened her, but she knew sometimes these things had to be. When she mentioned Will to her father, he'd said that in his opinion, Will Stearn was not a man to be ignored. 'And don't underestimate him, either,' he added. 'Could be folly.'

On the second afternoon, after collecting a new shirt and trousers from the mercantile, Will exercised his sorrel mare, rode it from the livery out to the old corrals, around the new rail yards down near the depot and back. At first dark, he took a walk that took him past the Henrys' clap-boarded house at the edge of town.

Rose, more conscious of Will's existence than she wanted to admit, had seen him coming, quickly contrived some shrub trimming in the small front yard.

Will smiled and took off his hat, revealing raw bruising, a wound above an eyebrow. There were still dark patches across his cheekbones, but his eyes were bright, creating the intelligent sparkle that had attracted her to him in the first place.

'Hello, Mr Stearn,' she said. 'What is it about this part of town that's caught your attention?' she asked.

'The doc's surgery. He wanted to keep an eye on my battle scars. Besides, it's away from the Bighorn Saloon . . . more peaceable like.'

'Well if that's the case, stop by a little later. Sometimes out here, you'd think the world had passed us by. I think some of these red blossoms are called sleepy hibiscus.'

Will gave a reserved, slightly amused smile, a parting nod. 'That sounds like a respectable invitation, ma'am. Perhaps I'll walk back this way. Good evening.'

He was already walking on when Rose continued. 'There was something else, Mr Stearn . . . another question. I did ask my father, but he didn't give me much of an answer.'

Will stopped and looked back at her. 'If I can help you, ma'am.'

Rose came to stand by the garden gate. The light dusk breeze whipped her hair back across her shoulders and Will smiled in approval.

'It's about that trouble you had with Mr Boe.'

'The trouble? You mean the fist fight?'

'Yes. Was it resolved?'

'With men like that, nothing's ever resolved,' Will said. 'Are you asking as a righteous campaigner, or is it a more personal concern?' he asked.

'Good gracious no.' Immediately, Rose looked discomfited. 'I'm simply curious. One moment you're causing disorder in our streets, next, you're using them for some sort of convalescence. I understood you were riding on.'

Will held her stare for a long moment. *Yeah, the straight and narrow way*, he thought, seeing the blush colours start to rise across her throat. 'Why don't you start calling me Will? At least, William?' he asked, increasing her embarrassment. 'There's a mid-west state where we'd be plighted with the kind of talk we're having.'

Feeling even more uncomfortable now, regretting that she had stopped him at all, Rose stepped back from the gate.

'Seriously, ma'am, and with respect, it's none of your business,' Will finally told her and walked off. 'That wasn't much of an answer, either,' he muttered.

Rose glared furiously after him until he went from sight. Then she turned back to the house, found her father standing in the doorway.

'Well, I've learned that deep down he's a regular peace-lover,' she said.

'You've learned nothing o' the sort, daughter,' Henry replied.

As she brushed past her father, Rose turned to see if she could still see Will, but he had already disappeared in the failing light.

'I only asked him what his intentions were . . . sort of. Why did he get so upset? I thought that's what men appreciated. Straight talking.'

Getting set for the late duty demands of Ragland, Henry buttoned up his jerga vest. 'A man busted up like he was, shouldn't rush things,' he replied. 'Anyway, what's it to you, really? Have I missed somethin'?

Rose looked surprised. 'Was he hurt that bad? Or are you making an excuse as to why he shouldn't already have left town?'

Henry shook his head. 'No Rose, I'm just sayin'. Why do you think he's hanging about?'

'His friend's starting up a business with Felix June. He wants to see him settled. I know that much.'

Henry pushed one of his many corncob pipes into a side pocket. 'But you've been thinkin' maybe it's some- thin' else keepin' him here,' he said. 'Clem Tapper's been workin' like a beaver on him an' June's business enterprise. He's not got the manpower or the money of Connie Boe, so he's doin' the building bits on a shoestring, apparently. I heard he's sent to New

Orleans for cookin' oil, an' other fancy foodstuffs. That's nothin' much for Stearn to get concerned about.'

Rose remained uneasy. 'Then what is it, Pa? There's *something* he wants,' she said.

'I told you. When he's fit, he'll ride. On the other hand, he could be waiting to have a fatal tryst with Newton Boe.'

Rose was now plainly shocked. 'Fatal for *him*. He'll get himself killed.'

'Likely,' Henry agreed, and started towards the street. 'Let's hope it's not tonight.'

Rose went after him and pulled him about face. She was angry now and confused. 'Then what are you waiting for? Boe to shoot him dead in the street, so you can say, 'I thought so'? I thought you were proud of this town ... the town that's getting itself civilized.'

Henry hitched his trousers, adjusted his gun belt. 'Rosie, you're old an' young at the same time, an' it's one hell of a job learnin' you without your ma. I can't stop this Will Stearn feller, no more than I can stop *you* when you've got a bee in your bonnet. If the man figures he owes Boe somethin' it's up to him how he goes about it. I'm a town sheriff, not a goddamn matchmaker.'

'If you know it's going to happen, one man against a whole gang of thugs *is* sheriff's work. What is it that Doctor Weaver says? 'Better a painful warning than painful treatment'?'

'An' pokin' your nose in, where an' when it's not wanted, is as good as signin' your own death warrant. I'll be home for supper usual time. What's on the table?'

'Don't go changing the subject, when you know I'm right.'

'When this place o' fine fixin's gets to open, maybe you'll have some competition, Rose. Maybe this ol' Tapper feller's got a new take on peachy pie. Maybe *that's* what's eatin' you. See you later.'

Out on the street, Henry stopped and took a long look around him. It was his responsibility for the lawful whims and actions of folk within the town's reach. And while Will Stearn decided to hang about in Ragland, *he* would have to be similarly looked out for.

As Henry approached the jailhouse, he started to sense trouble. At the moment it was sleeping, lurking around the corners, deep in the alleyways off the main street. And just beyond the other end of town, the bone yard was waiting. He knew that soon he would be signing the outlay for coffins and gravediggers. *Ride on, why don't you*, he thought. *Anywhere away from here.*

# 10

'Sorry, no credit,' Felix June told Newton Boe, and took back the bottle of aguardiente from the gunman's outstretched hand.

Boe's face instantly filled with anger. 'Hell, liquor boy, you know who I am. As soon as my wife starts up again, I'll have money enough to buy this whole goddamn dog hole.'

'Well let me tell you, Mr Boe, that's not exactly what me an' most o' the town have heard. Not that it's any of our business o' course, but if you've no cash or benefactor, you're nothin' more'n a vagrant.' June cursed inwardly, wondered how long he'd got to live.

As expected, Boe's reaction was immediate. As the man leaned forward again, June lifted the bottle from the counter and stacked it with others along the back bar.

This time, Rook leaned across the counter. 'You got some sand, mister, I'll say that. But why not think with your legs, an' give us the bottle? You'll get paid good enough.'

'Yeah, I'll tell that to my drummers. That should satisfy 'em,' June said. 'No money no drinks, is what it says above the door. So you might as well leave, 'cause I don't run a slate, either.'

Rook cursed openly. Newton Boe had already lost most of their Rojo Pluma takings, and the folk of Ragland were guarded. The cleaned-out pair couldn't even find a drunk to play penny ante.

'One last time, June. Are you goin' to give me back that bottle?' Boe was now pushing close to the bar, both hands on the counter, fingers outstretched.

June just shook his head. 'Make trouble in here an' you'll wind up in the jailhouse. Take a look around you. Some o' these fellers are just itchin' for the slightest excuse.'

Under the counter, June had his

hand around the butt of his big .44 Army Colt. 'Why don't you just up an' leave while you can still sit a saddle?' he warned.

Boe took a deep breath, straightened and glanced about the bar-room. Most of the men were either drinking, talking or looking at a hand of cards. But enough of them were watching what was going on up at the bar, even met Boe's cruel, grey eyes.

'OK,' he said. 'But remember who it was you refused a drink to. When the time's right, I'm comin' back to put a bullet in that bone head o' yours.'

'You do that an' you'll hang. There's still a public gallows in Los Alamos.' June kept his grip on the Colt, as he moved off along the bar.

'Hell, boss. Are you goin' to let that jumped-up whiskey peddler talk to you like that?' Rook said. 'We can take him an' all these dirt grubbers. Let's move on.'

Boe was back to glaring at Felix June again. 'Not right now,' he said. He was thrown at being got the better of, as a consequence didn't notice the man who had quietly moved in close behind them.

'Just keep your hands flat on the counter, Boe,' Will Stearn interrupted. 'Tell Rook to drop his gunbelt.'

Rook dropped a hand towards his gun butt, didn't quite make it before seeing the barrel of Will's Colt swing towards him.

'Unbuckle and step away. Clem Tapper couldn't make it on account of him not feeling so good. I told him it was OK, it's just between me and Boe.'

Boe stood completely still, but there was a glint of satisfaction in his eyes. 'Do as he says, Rook,' he said. 'He's not goin' to shoot a man in cold blood. He's got what they call principles. Let him have it his way.'

Nervously, Rook chewed at his bottom lip. He pulled at the buckle of his gunbelt, let the heavy holster crash to the floor. He stepped away, moving back to the crowd that were retreating to a safer distance.

Will stepped up close to Boe. 'You're going to regret laying your gun on me, Boe,' he said. 'Back off to the other end of the bar. You'll have a better chance than you gave me. Go.'

'You got some sort o' death wish, Stearn? *Chance* don't come into it.' Boe glanced at the tense, subdued on-lookers, took half-a-dozen steady paces backwards. 'I didn't figure you a rattle-brain, Stearn. Are you holdin' on to that gun, or are you goin' to die doin' the decent thing?'

'I'm giving you a fair chance,' Will said, and slowly put his Colt back in his holster. The silence in the room thickened as the two men stood facing each other.

'Yeah, give the audience a chance to see my work. Any time you like, Stearn,' Boe called.

Will felt a trickle of sweat high between his shoulder blades. But his nerves held as he waited for the slightest flinch from Boe.

'Hold it there, the pair o' you,' a voice barked. 'First to pull a gun, loses a leg . . . or an arm.'

Boe wheeled angrily, stared straight into the tight features of George Henry, the barrel of the sheriff's carbine.

Henry strode calmly forwards, allowed Boe the sight of his deputies who appeared in the swing-door space.

'It was Stearn who wanted this,' Boe snarled. 'He came in here shoutin' the odds . . . struttin' like a turkey cock.'

'I don't care. I won't stand for needless gunfights,' Henry said, moving between Will and Boe. 'I don't like bringin' my daughter into this, but she follows the doc's policy about prevention.'

'Keep your daughter out o' this,' Boe said. 'There's no need for me to retreat from a fair fight.'

'That's too bad.' Henry slashed his carbine across the counter. Shattered beer and whiskey glasses flew out across the bar, and the barrel-tip of his gun ended tight against Boe's chest. 'Don't make me go any further, Boe. I don't want to start enjoyin' my work,' he added.

Boe cursed in surprise, backed off a step. Rook moved back out of the crowd, started to come forward.

'That's far enough, Rook. Get back to where you're safe,' Henry told him. 'An' bein' someone who should take advice, I'd advise you to leave town . . . tonight.'

'You ain't needed here, Sheriff. It was Stearn who called the play.'

'An' I've just called this one,' Henry said, and motioned his deputies to step into the saloon.

Boe gave an evil grin, a low chuckle.

'What the hell's so goddamn funny, boss?' Rook asked.

'Him.' Boe pointed at Will. 'He comes in here as if he's grown horns, an' all the time knowin' it's a packed deal. Hah. Him an' sheriff must've spent a heap o' time workin' this one out.'

'Stearn had nothing to do with this,

Boe. I've been watchin' the both o' you.' Henry made clear. 'It was just a question o' when. But if you're both intent on spillin' blood, I'll put you somewhere real private to do it. So why not move out now an' avoid all that. Rook, you get lost with him, an' Stearn, you stay here until I say otherwise.'

Will gave Henry a challenging look, but the lawman showed little sign of unease or fear.

Boe knew he had to control himself. He didn't want to spoil his plans for moving in on his wife's interests before she'd got established. But he was still in big trouble. He had no resources, he couldn't frighten her, and she'd said she was through with him.

'Come on, Rook, let's go. Let's find some action away from this bunch o' stiffs,' he said. Boe pushed his way past Henry, sauntered boorishly from the saloon.

Henry went to the door, stood watching for a moment. Then he returned to the bar, snapped a coin on the counter and faced Will. 'I'm tellin' you this for your own good, Stearn. You've made your point, but I don't want you makin' it again. Next time it won't be a few booze glasses I smash open,' he said, and loud enough for most of the men in the bar-room to hear. He picked up the drink Felix June poured him, swallowed it in one. He gave Will a long steely look, before beckoning his deputies.

Out on the boardwalk, he looked thoughtfully into the darkness. *Yeah, you're out there somewhere, you son-of-a-bitch*, he thought.

'Boe's got no intention of leavin' town, an' neither has Stearn,' he told the deputies. 'From tomorrow, I'm goin' to need you men deputized proper . . . full time. That's not too many hours away, so go get your heads down for a while.'

The men agreed, nodded earnestly, and Henry sent them home. He turned up the street in the direction of his jailhouse, hoped the town would stay quiet until the saloon closed. After that, when liquor lost its hold and tempers simmered down, the night would take care of things in its usual way.

# 11

Will found Clem Tapper pacing backwards and forwards between the door and the window of their boarding-house room.

'Hell, I didn't think there was anythin' could put you off, Will,' Tapper said, as soon as Will returned. 'Not after what he did to you . . . to me.'

'How do you mean, put me off? Put me off what?'

'Henry told me about what happened in the saloon. I was goin' to come lookin' for you but thought better of it.'

'You're through with all that, looking after my back, Clem. I've had enough of Ragland and its idea of civic betterment. I'm riding on.'

'Yeah sure. But not right now?' Tapper studied Will for a short moment, then for a bit longer. 'You finally came to your senses, then?

George Henry said as much.'

'Henry said that? What the hell's he got to do with it?' Will questioned. 'Except that he's so set on getting me out of his hair, I wouldn't be surprised if he bushwhacked me in my bed.'

'It would certainly keep you quiet,' Tapper said, adding a curious, nervous grin.

'What about?'

'You know.'

'No, I don't think I do. Proved myself to Henry . . . come to my senses . . . keep me quiet? If you've got something in your craw, Clem, cough it up.'

'It's nothin', really.' Tapper looked at Will for another long time before he muttered. 'Agh, hell, you might as well know. There's talk you worked some-thin' out with him. They're sayin' he went along with it, because he'll do anythin' to stop a killin'. An' you because you're fearful o' Boe. That's what's goin' about, Will.'

'So what do you think, Clem old friend?'

'I've never been the one to do the thinkin', Will, you know that.' Tapper swallowed and turned away.

'So the town's decided. I run and you stay. Is that it, Clem?'

'I kind o' thought that's the way it was,' Tapper conceded. 'Me an' Felix will work somethin' out. But what about you?' he added uncomfortably. 'Maybe when you come back, I'll have a successful business . . . everythin' comfortable.'

Will studied his old partner, before pulling out his bag and tying-in his meagre belongings. 'Meantime, while you're serving up baked gopher, I'll be scuttling across the nearest desert, with my tail between my legs.' Coolly, Will pulled the door open.

'This isn't you runnin' out, is it Will?'

Will gave him no reply until he stepped into the passageway. 'Ask your friends,' he suggested bitterly and reached into his pocket.

'Hell, forget money,' Tapper snapped. 'I've still got more'n three hundred left.

If you're really goin', don't make too many enemies an' stay on the lookout.'

'Yeah I will. An' you remember there's nothing worse than stewed gravy,' Will muttered and closed the door behind him. Cursing silently, he walked out to the back staircase of the building, and down to the yard. From there, he went straight to the livery stable and paid off the stabling bill for his sorrel.

Fifteen minutes later, he led the mare back to the boarding-house yard. In the shadowless gloom he hitched the horse to the brake handle of a delivery cart, glancing up to see Tapper's room light was still on. 'Probably missing me already,' he muttered, and turned towards the main street.

Stepping on to the boardwalk, he was instantly confronted by George Henry. The sheriff had been waiting, leaning against an overhang post sucking on a corncob pipe.

'At least you're saddled up,' he drawled.

'Yeah, you don't miss much, do you, Sheriff?' Will returned.

'Not a lot. So why aren't you ridin' out like we agreed? Forget somethin'?'

'I guess you could say that. If I did, it's my business.'

Henry shook his head. 'This time o' night, it's mine, feller. Come mornin' I want to know you're a good few hours gone. How many more times you got to be told?'

Will looked both ways into the darkness up and down the street, put the palm of his hand to the butt of his Colt.

'Look, I've already stopped you gettin' killed once tonight,' Henry rasped. 'I don't intend to spend any more time . . . can't be *bothered* spendin' any more time on it.'

'You weren't asked to, Sheriff. Leave me be.'

'It's my *job* goddamnit. Keepin' the peace is what they pay me for. Men with guns aren't welcome on these streets, an' that goes for you as much as

118

for Newton Boe. Now, I've given orders for you to clear this town.'

'Or else? Threats usually carry an upshot, Sheriff.'

'Oh, that's for me to know, Stearn . . . my advantage.'

Will gave him an intense look, then turned away. 'I'm going to see Clem Tapper, before I go anywhere.'

'You've already seen him. He called you gritless . . . chicken. Probably didn't use them words, but the juice was there, an' you've been thinkin' on it. Put's a whole new motive on leavin' town, eh? You never struck me as someone flawed with the burden o' pride, Stearn.'

Will walked off, ignoring Henry. But he knew the lawman would be tagging him, would be until he cleared the streets of Ragland. He was about to turn back, have a few more testy words, when there was a sudden eruption of noise from down the street. Instinctively, he moved from the middle of the boardwalk, allowed Henry to appear beside him.

The doors of the Rojo Pluma flew open, and with the spilling light, Connie Boe came staggering out. She ran into the low railing, turned and dropped to the boards, her back to the street. Before she regained her footing, Henry was cursing, breaking into a lumbering run to find out what was happening.

'Goddamn you, Newt. I'll finish you for this,' Connie Boris fumed. '*Cerdo feo*,' she added, almost spitting the words.

Newton Boe appeared in the doorway. '*You* said we were through, an' *I'm* makin' it official,' he rasped. 'Take your baubles an' get the hell out.'

'The Rojo Pluma belongs to me. You've no claim on it, legal or otherwise.' Connie Boe stretched a hand to the railing and pulled herself upright.

'See her off the property,' Boe rasped, taking a step back inside.

Hoke Plantin and Rook came out, straightaway went to carry out Boe's bidding.

But Connie Boe was in no mood to be manhandled. She struck out at

Plantin, but Rook stepped forward quickly and slapped her hard across the face.

'Back off,' Henry yelled, as she fell forward, on to her knees. 'You lay a hand on her again, an' I'll forget I'm a lawman.'

The gunhand swung about. His lips tightened around stained teeth, and his eyes were suddenly bright with fight lust. When he saw Henry levering a shell into a carbine, his aversion to lawmen provoked him into action. He dropped his right shoulder and pulled his Colt.

'Take him, Rook,' Boe goaded. 'It's what you've wanted.'

Rook fired and his bullet chewed into the flesh of Henry's left shoulder. The lawman went spinning back against the overhang post, but he didn't go down. Gripping the carbine he hooked his right arm around the post and swerved from the boardwalk to the darkness of the street.

Plantin and Rook both opened fire.

In the darkness, their bullets splintered the upright, then pocked the solid dirt of the street.

'You wouldn't want me to leave town just yet, would you, Sheriff?' Will shouted as he drew his revolver.

Plantin backed off, still firing but more random, glancing for the protection of the Rojo Pluma. Newton Boe was stamping forward, clasping his big Colt in the relative steadiness of a two-handed grip.

'Shoot him, goddamnit,' Will yelled, and, from a kneeling position in the street, Henry fired his carbine one-handed from the hip.

Will fired low at Plantin. He saw his bullet hit him in the leg and turned his attention to Rook.

'We're not in a good place, boss,' Rook yelled above the roar of the gunfire.

Boe took a daring step forward. 'Get back inside,' he commanded. 'You too, Hoke.'

Will and the sheriff stopped firing,

watched apprehensively as the three gunhands, shoulder-to-shoulder, retreated into the Rojo Pluma.

'Some other time, that sight would be real amusing,' Will shouted at Connie Boe, who returned a thin, fearful smile.

Plantin lurched inside and started to refill the cylinder of his gun. Rook followed, and Boe kicked the doors shut.

'We can hold 'em off from in here until they get reasonable,' Boe said.

'Until we figure out what to do next, you mean,' Plantin rasped. 'In a couple o' minutes we'll be makin' our own last stand.'

The noise of the shooting was drawing people in faltering haste along the street. Grimacing, George Henry stepped back up to the boardwalk, and Will helped Connie Boe to her feet.

'It seems we have something in common, Mrs Boe . . . Connie,' he said.

'But nothing you'd want to be remembered for. This is the second time you've come to my assistance.'

'Well, you never actually fired me, as

I recall. I took payment, so technically, I'm still in your employ.'

'That husband o' yours won't get away with this, Mrs Boe,' Henry declared. 'There's rights an' wrongs, so if you want this place back . . . '

'Oh yes, Sheriff, I don't recall wanting anything more in my life. And the last thing Newton Boe ever gets from me will be his gravestone,' she vowed, regaining some composure. 'Furthermore, I might go back to being Connie Moss.'

# 12

Clem Tapper came at an ungainly run from the boarding-house, didn't stop until he was standing between Will and George Henry.

'Hell, I knew it had to be you,' he panted. 'Hope this weren't on my account.'

'Well, it wasn't that I was getting bored,' Will replied, a little sharper than he meant.

'Keep out o' this, Tapper,' Henry warned. 'Just one o' you two's enough trouble.'

'*You* keep out of it,' Tapper retorted. 'Your escapade in the Bighorn's made it sound like Will's someone who turns away from a fight. Well, mister, you were wrong, an' so's the scuttlebutt from folk who saw. Will Stearn's a law abidin' citizen. There's a difference, goddamnit.'

'You ol' fool. You think I don't know that?' Henry snapped back. 'I've wire checked on him . . . both o' you.'

Will allowed his jaw to drop while Henry wiped sweat from his face. Connie Boe seemed to be the one least affected by the trouble.

'What exactly *did* you find out about him, Sheriff?' she asked. 'Something you can share?'

'Nary a whit, ma'am,' Henry said. 'Right now you should be concerned about where you're spendin' the rest of the night. In the mornin', if you need any help in decidin' what grievances to level at Newton Boe . . . your husband, I'll be more'n happy to give advice.'

'Thank you, Sheriff, I'll take you up on that. As for the next few hours, and if there's room, the boarding-house will do fine.'

'An' you needn't worry about your girls, ma'am,' Tapper said. He nodded towards the Rojo Pluma, where the girls, in an assortment of bright dresses, were being ushered rudely on to the boardwalk.

The moment they saw Connie, they

all began talking at once, hurrying excitedly towards their employer.

Connie held up her hand and smiled. 'Quiet,' she said. 'I look like the mother hen. Esther, you're the most level-headed. Do you know what's happening?'

Esther blinked at the unexpected compliment. She was without her working masque, clear-faced, looked younger. 'Not really,' she answered uncertainly. 'But Mr Boe told us to say that if you try to get back the Rojo Pluma he'll fight all of you that's here. He's going to open for business with or without you. If you don't agree . . . anyone tries to break in, he'll shoot them down. Then he'll get more men an' wreck the town. I think that's what he said.' Esther was visibly upset, close to tears as she finished the message.

Henry cursed and Tapper shook his head. Will stared thoughtfully at the closed doors of the Rojo Pluma.

'There was a message for you too, Mr Stearn,' Esther continued.

'Yeah, don't worry, miss. I can guess

what it was,' Will said, nodding recognition of Esther's concern.

Henry was about to lurch into another angry outburst, when his daughter appeared out of the darkness. 'I'll head her off,' he muttered. But he accepted he couldn't, and cursed quietly.

'What's going on now, Pa?' Rose demanded.

'Mrs Boe has just left her establishment . . . forcibly. It's nothin' for you to get agitated about, Rose. Maybe somethin' less.'

Rose knew her feelings were irrational, that she had no actual reason for disliking Connie Boe. But it bothered her that she moved freely in the world of men; it twisted her emotions. 'Well how much of a loss is that, when you've already closed the place?' she said, casting a glance at the customarily scarlet-dressed woman.

Connie Boe decided to take a few steps towards them. 'You have a point there, little Miss Henry. But it's a shame you don't understand more,' she said. 'The Rojo Pluma might be closed, and Newton Boe might burn it to the ground. But it still belongs to me, and I'm not giving it up. Not without a fight. That means there's going to be a heap of unrest, so maybe you and your gentle, sensitive friends should stay away.'

With that, Connie motioned her girls towards the boarding-house. 'Mr Stearn, me and the girls are relocating. If they'll take us in, will you join me . . . us, for a drink?' she asked, so that most of those gathered about could hear.

As if in response to Rose Henry's huffy intake of breath, Will smiled. 'Yeah, why not? It should be safe enough,' he said. 'Besides, I won't be leaving town tonight, after all. Not now I'm a guardian angel of its sheriff.'

Henry glared furiously. 'I owe you that, Stearn,' he rasped. 'Just don't push it . . . stay out o' my hair.'

Will went off with Connie and her girls. Tapper watched with interest before deciding to tag along.

'Pa, are you going to tolerate this?' Rose Henry snorted.

'Tolerate what? The man's been invited for a drink . . . a private affair. What in tarnation's got into you lately, girl?'

Rose pointed to the boarding-house. 'That. All those people *and* Mr Stearn. I mean, how big can the rooms be? It's going to be like a cow barn in there . . . a threat to public health.'

Henry wiped more sweat from his face and sighed resignedly. 'That's one way o' lookin' at it. Some would see it as hittin' the jackpot.' He took his daughter by the arm and steered her off. 'It's time you grew up, Rose. I think I'll have to see about gettin' you a little down-to-earth learnin',' he said quietly.

Rose pulled clear and issued a vinegary oath.

'Ain't heard that in a while,' Henry muttered through an incredulous grin.

Rose's flouncy departure halted anything more specific Henry had to say.

He looked intently after his daughter, then back to the boarding-house. *She's growin' up*, he thought. *An' if I didn't know any better, I'd say she's just discovered jealousy.*

* * *

Connie Boe looked with distaste at the room's basic furnishings. She poured Will a generous whiskey before settling herself on the edge of one of two single beds. 'I wouldn't allow my dog to live in this . . . if I had one,' she said, controlling any deeper opinion of her surroundings.

'Did you have anything in mind by inviting me for this drink?' Will asked.

'It's not often that I have *nothing* in mind. Have you changed your mind about not leaving town right away?'

'No, I'm OK for the moment. But I'm guessing that staying here any longer might depend on you,' Will said, calmly took a cautious sip of his boarding-house whiskey.

Connie leant towards him. 'George Henry mentioned that you had a dirt-free past.'

Will shook his head. 'He said he couldn't find anything. And I can't be the only one who's riding with that ticket.'

'Hmm. Well, I don't know who they are. Especially those who are up to overseeing the Rojo Pluma. I've had Owen Hunston for more years than I can remember, but even loyalty runs its course. That's why I want to talk to you.'

Will finished his drink, held out his glass for a refill. 'If that's some sort of business offer you're making, aren't you being a tad hopeful?'

'Why don't you call me Connie? For heaven's sake, you've earned the right. As for being hopeful, I'll be getting my place back, have no fear about that. And when I do, I want someone to look after it . . . my interests. That person would be keeping an eye on just about everything, even the girls. You, Mr Will

Stearn, have the credentials I'm looking for. Does a quarter share interest you?'

Will looked surprised, but didn't show as to specifically what. 'That's buying a man high, isn't it?' he asked. 'You could hire a troop of Range Riders for that sort of reward.'

'Or the whole of the Mexican Army. But that doesn't mean they'd be any good at it. To begin with, you'd have to deal with Newton Boe, and you know how much of a test that's going to be. Right now, you're biding your time, Will, and we both know what for. Like we both know what else is keeping you here. I'm not blind, feller.'

'Not blind? Are you seeing something I'm not?'

'Miss Honeysuckle, Rose Henry. I've seen the way you catch her eye, the way she catches yours. So think about it. I'm offering the chance of a good job with good money and prospects. And just in case you're worried about whether the Rojo Pluma's a fit place for human habitation, don't. Once I've cleared out the problem of rat infestation, the place will be as pure as a nun's heart. What do you say?'

Will slowed up on his drinking as he thought, gave Connie the time to maintain her offer.

'The only objection I can see is if you've already decided to try your luck someplace else,' she continued. 'Maybe you want to round up cows . . . settle dust with spit instead of Bourbon. Maybe you'd like to swing a hammer along the railroad spur. Maybe you're wanting to launch your own competition?'

Will turned to face her, his forehead set in a frown. He was unsure if Connie Boe's proposal was the whiskey stretching his imagination. 'No hitches? A straight business, working deal?' he said.

'Dealing with Newt might be a bit twisty. But once he's out of circulation there'll be no other partner, matrimonial or business. Men are allowed to be loners outside the custom, why not me? I can have the papers drawn up in the morning, and I'll put in a proviso. If you die in the carrying out of your duties, anything owed gets paid to whoever you want.'

Will picked up his hat and fitted it to his head, gave Connie the empty glass. 'Right now, my life's just about the only thing I've got to lose,' he said brusquely. 'So with you taking care o' that, why not? I'll sign tomorrow.'

Connie was smiling cheerfully when she escorted him to the door. 'There's a big gain, Will . . . getting well-to-do in a year. It's up to you. Good night. Oh, in the morning, I'll let it be known you left here after a single neighbourly drink,' she added with a wink and a knowing smile.

Will grinned, nodded at the girls who were mingling in the corridor, exchanging funny stories about their accommodation. He made his way downstairs to find Clem Tapper waiting up for him.

Tapper looked at his friend for a long moment. 'Fightin' over you, were they?' he asked.

'No, they're outside waiting for you to let them in here. We're all glad you didn't.' Will dragged off his boots. 'I've been offered a job,' he said wearily, a few moments later. He toppled sideways on to his narrow bed, yawned and closed his eyes. 'Good one too . . . a big improvement on our usual fifty goddamn cents a day.'

# 13

Clem Tapper couldn't turn off from the night's disorder. In the early hours, he was up and dressed, making his way quietly down the steps to the building's back yard. He walked the town, went to the corrals to look at the horses. His claybank wasn't particularly interested in seeing him, and he decided to find somewhere with coffee. A half hour later he was back at the boarding-house, where there was some activity in and around the kitchen. Entering through the back door, he was surprised to see Connie Boe talking with the cook.

'Harder to find than a mutton puncher from Texas,' Clem chipped in casually.

'What is?' the cook asked.

'Strong, hot coffee.'

'Hah. My gran'-mammy used to say

that good coffee should be as hot as Romeo's breath, an' as strong as his arms.' The cook pointed to the stove. 'Help yourself,' he offered.

The two old men chuckled and Connie smiled indulgently. 'And here's to us,' she said, raising her cup to Tapper. 'First toast of the day.'

'First toast? Us? I'm not with you.'

'Me and Will. Didn't he tell you? We're partners. Well, will be in a few hours.'

Tapper almost dropped the coffee pot as he cursed, turned to stare at Connie. 'Hell, he said he'd been offered a job . . . didn't mention *you* though. He said nothin' about partners either. You an' him?'

'Yep, that's it. He agreed on a quarter share. I'd say he's making a wise move. A shack load of money nearer the start of your life's a tad smarter than at the other end. Don't you think, Clem?'

'Yeah. Not the same for a big mis-take, though. Will don't usually throw in with anyone who offers easy riches.'

'Ain't that the truth,' Connie responded with an ironic smile. 'Look Clem, you might as well get it into your head, Will Stearn's now working for me.'

'Ain't that stretchin' the term 'partners' a bit in the wrong direction?' Tapper said. 'What do you reckon he's workin' as?' he demanded.

'My house manager. He'll be there to keep troublemakers from my front door.'

'What the hell front door's that? The way I hear it, your gunny husband ain't ready to let you or anyone else back in. You ain't got a pot to piss in, lady.'

'That's up until now. Will's going to make him . . . force his hand.'

Tapper carried his coffee can across the room, angrily confronted the woman at closer range. 'You see here, Mrs Boe, or whatever name you're usin' today, why don't you back off? Will's good, but he's no match for Boe, an' his cronies. You know it.'

'I don't know any such thing. 'Specially if what I've seen and heard so far is anything to go by,' Connie replied with a cool smile.

'Well, the way things are set up right now you wouldn't, would you. If Boe was that serious about takin' over your joint, how come he hasn't already skinned you? I'd say all your shenanigans out front was lies. I'd even say you were behind that goddamn card game . . . got clever-mouthed to stall off George Henry. Yeah, I can see it now. I don't trust you further'n I can spit. Once upon a time I did . . . now I don't.'

Connie studied him sourly for a moment, then tilted her head back, let the derision break open. 'If that's your opinion of me, perhaps it's better you keep it to yourself. Especially until me and Will get our partnership made official. Yeah? You think you can mind your own business that long?' she snapped. 'Will's given me his word and I happen to think he'll stick to it.' She finished her coffee and nodded her thanks to the cook. She moved to the door, careful to embrace herself in her blanket wrap.

The cook watched her eagerly, and Tapper watched the cook. 'You want to look out for that one,' he said as the door closed behind her. He placed the remains of his coffee on the stove. 'You must've been a real disappointment to your gran'-mammy,' he muttered and stomped from the kitchen.

Will was lying back with his eyes open, staring up at the ceiling when Tapper returned.

'What the hell's eating you, Clem?' he asked as soon as Tapper was through the door. 'It must be something to get you up at the crack of dawn.'

'That woman . . . Connie Boe. I hear you're teamin' up with her.'

'Oh? And who told you that?'

'She did. Hell, Will, I don't ever tell you what to do or who to be friendly with. But this time I've got to make an exception . . . got to. I know she's been thrown out o' towns like this a dozen times over, an' until now I always thought it was some sort of approval. But if you think about it, can all them town bigwigs, as well as ordinary folk, have been wrong, an' she's been right? Hell no.'

Will shrugged and kicked back the sheets. 'There's a first time for everything, Clem.' He got up and poured water in the corner washstand. After a sluice and enthusiastic splutter, he pulled on his clothes and buckled on his gunbelt.

'Where are you goin' now?' Tapper asked.

'Out . . . got things to do.'

'All of a sudden you treatin' me like a rough steer?'

'You've got stuff to set up with Felix June. So far, I've been offered employment as a bouncer with Connie Boe. If what you're really worried about's getting smeared by association, I'll get a room at the end of the corridor.'

Tapper looked hurt. 'Ah, hell there's no need for that, Will. If you can put up with me, I can do the same for you . . . always have done. I'm lookin' out for you, goddamnit.'

'It's a lot more than that, Clem.' Will closed the door after him as he went out.

Tapper stood cursing to himself, the resentment towards Connie building inside him. He felt that she had used her eye-catching guise to entice Will into service; that Will would take his fight to Newton Boe, despite the added threat of Plantin and Rook.

Five minutes later, Tapper had made up his mind about what he was going to do. He dragged his own gunbelt from deep in his old canvas war bag and strapped it high and tight around his waist. It had been a long time since he had worn a gun, and now it felt heavy and awkward on him. It was only when he was certain that Will had left the boarding-house that he walked thought-fully downstairs, out to the main street.

★   ★   ★

Will took a half-hearted swipe at the sleepy hibiscus blossoms as he approached the front door of the sheriff's house. He was greeted by George Henry himself. The man was hatless and shirtless, but wore his old Colt.

Henry took a seasoned corncob pipe from his mouth. 'What is it now, Stearn?' he scowled. 'You come to cast your crooked shadow across my property?'

'No, Sheriff, that certainly wasn't my intention. It's to do with there being a change in my prospects. If you'd like to take a walk down to that jailhouse of yours, there's some papers need signatures.'

Before Henry had time to say anything, Will continued. 'I'm entering a partnership with Connie Boe . . . a sort of top hand. It's one way of gaining the right to stay here . . . keeping my name off the vagrancy roll. Who can handle this sort of thing?'

'If you mean qualified to witness a signature, it's usually a doctor or bank manager. My office has been known to handle it, on occasion. But I'm not sure we're gettin' this right. A tag for the right to stay in town ain't the same as permission for a gunfight with Newton Boe. Is that what this is about, Stearn? Makin' your showdown lawful?'

'I guess it's about some sort of justice, Sheriff,' Will accepted. 'Do you remember last night . . . Boe shooting it out with you . . . him only backing off when it got too hot and witnesses appearing? Do you remember that?'

Henry rubbed a hand slowly across his face. 'Christ, Stearn, I'm gettin' too old for this,' he started.

Then it was Rose's voice. 'Who's that you're talking to, Pa?' she called.

'Will Stearn. He's come to see me about somethin'.'

'Talking of shadows . . . ' Will muttered under his breath, thinking he heard a groan of disappointment from inside the house.

Next moment, Rose Henry was standing in the doorway. Her long raven hair was pulled back tight and she looked bright and sharp. But not even the distrustful look in her eyes could lessen the effect she had on Will. He recalled Connie's words of the previous night, thought he'd probably have to ask for more clarification.

'Morning, Rose,' he said, with a short tug at the brim of his hat. 'Sorry to disturb you.'

Rose nodded a curt greeting and turned away. 'I'll get your breakfast, Pa. You're not leaving the house until you've eaten . . . not for any reason,' she said.

'I wish there was someone to tell *me* that,' Will muttered with a wry smile. 'I'd sort of like it to be the bank manager, Myles Brick, for the signing of those papers, Sheriff. But either you or the doctor . . . there's no hurry.'

At the gate, Will turned, looked up quickly as he clipped the latch over the post. Rose was standing at a front window watching him. He returned a warm smile, but it wasn't reciprocated.

He was still smiling as he walked back into the town, enjoying the cool of the early morning. An hour after daybreak, breezes would start to scoot hot and dry along the main street, later, sear anything under their touch. But the heat would be of little consequence to Will's agenda. He used the quiet boardwalk on the Bighorn side of the street, to ponder his predicament. Lawfully installed in the Rojo Pluma, he would see to it the establishment was run properly. Then, if things went well, perhaps he could raise a stake. Perhaps enough to buy a productive section. *And perhaps I should keep that goddamn bank manager in the blend*, he thought, facetiously. But before any of that could happen, there was the ominous and sure-fire problem of Newton Boe.

Will glanced through the saloon's open doors. He thought an early gut settler would go down nicely, but changed his mind on seeing Felix June swabbing the gummy puncheons.

Heading back to alert Connie regarding his arrangement with George

Henry, Will was turning into the lodgings when a single gunshot broke the morning quiet. He touched the butt of his gun with the palm of his hand, stood listening to the echo as it winged its way towards him from the direction of the Rojo Pluma.

Cursing, instinct stung him into a run. More shots followed, and less than thirty yards ahead he saw Clem Tapper lurch from the alleyway alongside the Rojo Pluma. Tapper was twisting around, trying to fire behind at his pursuers, but Will saw his body get hammered with bullets. Tapper was trying to turn into the comparative safety of the main street. He staggered, fell to his knees, tried to rise, coughed and fell in the sunlit dirt.

Will took a deep breath, drew his Colt and steadied himself, guessing, hoping as to what would happen next.

'Goddamn you sons-of-bitches,' he said, hissing the words when Rook and Hoke Plantin showed themselves.

As the pair ran to Tapper's body, Will

called and fired. His bullet hit Rook full in the chest, the second, smashing home within an inch of the first. The gunhand stepped backwards, yelled at Plantin for help, but that was all. He smacked up against the corner wall of the building and collapsed, dead before he hit the ground.

Plantin shot at Will as he regained the alleyway. Will fired, but he was too hasty, his blood was hot and he was letting anger take over. He ran forward, swore savagely as Plantin dived into the side doorway of the Rojo Pluma.

He thought about following, kicking the door in, but he heard a low groan from Tapper. 'Hell, Clem, I thought you were dead,' he muttered and pushed his Colt back into his holster. He held Tapper as gently as he could, dragged him a few feet to the cover of a stone water trough. He saw two, maybe three bloody wounds in the front, guessed there was another in the old-timer's back.

'You got enough holes to be dead,' he

told him. 'Let's rest up here a bit.'

Sweat ran across Tapper's weather-worn features and blood trickled from the corner of his mouth. 'All I'm good for's gettin' you into trouble, Will,' he rasped, ground his jaw against the hurt. 'Ride on now. I won't look. I'll close my eyes . . . make it easy. Go on, git.'

'When we've got you looked at, I promise. A few minutes from now you won't see my dust.' Even as he spoke, Will heard noise, some movement from inside the front of the Rojo Pluma. He drew his Colt with his right hand, took a few paces back and stooped to pick up Tapper's revolver in his left. He glared up at the doors in front of him, almost prayed for someone to emerge.

'Can you hear me, Stearn?' a voice called from further up the street. 'If ol' Tapper's still breathin', get him back here.'

Will took a sideways glance. He saw George Henry lumbering quickly towards him, the short barrel of his carbine catching the low sun as it made its first appearance at the eastern end of the main street. Then he was back to glaring at the Rojo Pluma, his eyes taking in everywhere, alert for any sign of movement.

'Is he hurt bad?' Henry stood a couple of paces from Will, his carbine tracing a line across the front of the building. 'It don't look like he's settin' to walk away,' he added.

Will looked down at his trail friend, and wretchedness suddenly touched him. 'Yeah. It's about as bad as hurt gets,' he agreed. 'But he's not dying out here in the street, goddamnit. You keep them dogs penned inside. I'll *carry* him to the doc's if I have to.'

'No, leave him be. Doc's right behind. I told him to come runnin' at the sound o' gunfire.'

Will looked up. He saw Doc Weaver coming from the direction of the jailhouse, Felix June arriving from the Bighorn. His hands were still wet with dirty water, hanging useless at his sides as he looked down on his new buddy and would-be business partner.

Tapper was lying very still, blinking back the pain that racked his body. 'Connie Boe,' he mumbled, his grip tightening on Will's wrist. 'I had it wrong, Will. That husband o' hers wants her dead so's he can make legal on this place . . . money, if there is any.'

'Yeah, I know that, Clem. It must have riled him, finding out I'm full square in the way.'

The doctor indicated for Will to move aside. He hunkered down, looked closely at Tapper's face. He attempted to unbutton and lift away the bloody shirt, but instead shook his head and got to his feet.

'I've nothing to repair these injuries with, Mr Stearn. I've got laudanum, but I doubt it would have time to work.'

Will took a deep, affecting breath. 'He never wanted much. A bit of luck just now and again would have been fair,' he said quietly.

Clem Tapper's eyes closed. He almost smiled, as if Will had said something he agreed with.

'You've been in this town some time, Sheriff,' Will said, turning to George Henry. 'Can you remember a time when you felt safe?'

'Nope, not if truth were told. I remember tellin' Rose she was, when her ma died. How about you?'

'I said it to Clem before we rode in.'

Henry considered Will's caustic reply, gave a long, thoughtful look down at Tapper. 'So, there'll be nothin' to keep you here,' he stated flatly.

'Oh, there is. It's like being a kid . . . getting to the end of your lemon sugar.' Will nodded at the Rojo Pluma. 'We've got the best bit penned in there. The bit that makes it all meaningful.'

# 14

Will let it be known that mourners and grievers would be strangers and would have embarrassed Clem Tapper. So he buried his old friend in the sole company of Felix June.

Will suspected that June had more than trail dust in his eye as they rode back to town. 'Sure makes you think about stuff,' he said as they drew up near the jailhouse.

'Yeah,' June answered distractedly. 'I was thinking back to when you an' Clem rode into town. You trusted no one, an' Clem everyone, or so it seemed. I liked him straight off . . . easy company, you know. You make many acquaintances in my line o' business, but few friends. Nothin' for more than a day or two. With Clem I thought there was somethin' better . . . certainly somethin' more interestin' than pourin' drunk water. He told me he'd be glad when he was shot o' you. Ha, I think he meant he could go it alone. Are you stayin' here in Ragland, or are you ridin' on?'

'I told Clem I was riding on. But that was when he was alive.'

June nodded, then went on dourly. 'I'm not exactly a pistolero, Will, but I've got a piece of ordnance that make's one hell of a noise. If I can be of any help in takin' out Boe . . . '

Will slipped down from the saddle, nodded at George Henry who was standing in the doorway of the jail-house. After hitching his sorrel mare to the tie-rail, he turned back to June.

'Thank you, Felix. I understand what you're saying . . . and why. I'm sure you'll know if and when I need you.'

June carried on down the street towards the Bighorn. Will watched him thoughtfully, waited until he'd gone inside the saloon before looking to Henry.

'Mrs Boe is waitin' and so's Myles

Brick,' the sheriff said. 'If you still want it done. Are you OK?'

'Yeah, I'm just fine. The sooner we get it settled the better all round,' Will said and stepped inside.

Henry closed the door and motioned for Will to take a seat close to the desk.

Myles Brick was writing swiftly on a single-sheeted document, and he didn't look up when Will sat down.

*Yeah I don't like you either, feller,* Will was thinking as the bank manager mumbled something about not being more than a minute.

Brick wrote a final line, then scanned the page from start to finish. He sat up, smiled his unemotional smile. 'Well, that should satisfy the both of you. But before we get to signing, I'm delighted you're taking up this offer, Mr Stearn. Ragland needs an attraction. Unfortunately, the Rojo Pluma has acquired a notorious reputation of late, so I have suggested, and Mrs Boe agrees, that a start-over name would be in order,' he said. 'So, the man who manages The

Even Break will require integrity, drive and temperament.' With that assertion, Brick offered Will the document.

Yep, a real creepy opportunist, Will confirmed to himself. *But you were right about Clem not being much of a long term investment*, he thought bitterly. His distaste for Myles Brick grew as he realized that if Clem had been given the loan he'd asked for, he'd probably still be alive. And he, Will, would have left town.

'Ladies first. Let Mrs Boe read it,' he said sharply.

Brick shrugged, handed the paper to Connie who read the last sentence, before handing it across to Will.

Will took his time reading over what he thought were important clauses. He lifted a dipping pen from the ink pot and signed his name at the foot of the page.

'I'm sorry about Clem,' Connie said, after she too had signed. 'I guess age and patience don't mix.'

'Yeah. He didn't know what he was

up against . . . that it wasn't worth dying for.'

'I know. Silly ol' fool comes to mind.'

'He'd got *you* checked out. He said you were on the level, so not quite so foolish,' Will replied. 'That's the reason I just signed. Now, if you'll excuse me, there's someone I must go and see.'

Uncertainly, Myles Brick rose to his feet. George Henry shifted forward.

'Are you goin' to accompany us?' he asked.

A flush of alarm coloured the banker's features. 'No. I'll leave that to a more appropriate authority. I want to get somewhere other than the local cemetery.'

'Then you'd better scuttle off. Consider your fee, when you're safe behind those big bank doors,' Will grated. Then he studied Henry for a moment. 'Sounds like you're coming with me?' he said.

'No, son, it's the other way round. I'm peace officer to this town an' get paid to try an' keep it. Newton Boe shot dead an old man. I'll take him in for that.'

Will nodded, suddenly felt he better understood the sheriff's position. 'I hope that doesn't mean you're going to deputize me?'

Henry shook his head. 'I got a feelin' you'd resist. Got any objections to stormin' the barricades?'

'Yeah, one or two immediately come to mind.'

Henry frowned. 'Like what?' he asked.

Will looked at Connie. 'There's one door in front, and one on the side. There's got to be another.'

'There was one at the back, off the utility room, but I had it boarded up. I didn't like the idea of anyone slipping in behind me.'

Will smiled. 'Yeah, I can imagine.'

'What sort o' boarded up?' Henry asked.

'The real safe and sound sort.'

'Then Boe's got enough men in there to keep guard.'

'Enough men? Who else has he got with him, besides Plantin?' Will asked.

'Hunston. I haven't seen him for a while. How about you, Mrs Boe . . . Connie?'

'I've no reason to suspect he'd walk out on me, so I don't think he's in there pondering on which side his bread's buttered. Besides, he's no gunhand.'

'No, but he'd make noise . . . help 'em, involuntarily.'

'How'd he do that?'

'By Boe shoving a gun barrel into his regions. A sort of bargaining device. And expendable.'

Connie gave Henry a glance, nodded reluctantly. 'He's probably got them shaking scared.'

'And that makes it a dangerous place,' Will added. 'I'm for getting Boe's attention, while I make a run for Plantin. If I can take *him* out, it'll be just Boe and me. That's what he wants . . . what he's going to get.'

Henry moved about the office mumbling agitatedly to himself. 'My way's old school. Me an' the deputies shootin' the place down around 'em. Make it so close to hell, they'll all want to die outside.'

'Stylish, Sheriff, I'll say that. But remember the story of rats in a flour-sack. It's the last one out that bites.'

'Yeah. That'll be Newton Boe. I'll be chasin' Plantin who'll likely make a run for it.'

Concern touched Connie's already drawn features. 'It'll never happen like that. It's not in Newt's nature to surrender, and when he thinks he's lost, he'll take down as much as he can, any way he can. As for Plantin, he won't run. He knows Newt will shoot him dead if he so much as looks the other way.' She moved away from the table, followed Henry's walkabout. 'I don't want killing . . . needless bloodshed. Last night I was mad enough to agree to anything, but imagine if innocent people got hurt. I think we should try and come to an arrangement. If need be, I'll buy him off.'

Despite being brusquely dismissed, Myles Brick had remained standing in the jailhouse doorway. 'Maybe you should have done that when he first got here,' he said. 'Now he's going to up the stake, and you won't have enough.'

'He'll accept if he thinks it's all I've got. If it's everything.'

'But it won't be everything. Things have changed,' Will interrupted. 'I'm a part owner of what he wants, and with Clem's death, I've suddenly become a ground blizzard. He won't rest until he sees my toes pointing north. That was going to be the message from young Esther . . . what I've got to see him about.'

'I can't let you do it, Stearn,' Henry snapped. 'I didn't before an' I'm not now.'

'You did what any self-respecting peace officer would have done,' Will said. 'Why not let me do the same.'

* ★ *

162

In the ensuing silence, while options were sinking in, Will had got to wondering when Henry's daughter was going to turn up when there was a tentative knock.

Rose pushed against the part-opened jailhouse door. She saw the gathering inside and instinctively drew back.

'Ah daughter, come in. You might as well add your dime's worth,' her father called out. 'Right now, you're as level-headed as most folk in this town . . . maybe more so.'

'The Santa Fe Flyer,' Will muttered.

'What?' Henry said.

'Like the Santa Fe Flyer,' Will repeated with a cynical smile. 'A head of steam and on time.'

Rose delayed in the doorway a moment, then, mentioning the heat, partly closed the door behind her. 'I don't know that I can add anything, but I do have an opinion on what you're probably all up to,' she said.

Henry explained the whole problem to her, wasn't much surprised when she showed irritation at the partnership between Will and Connie Boe. 'So what is your opinion?' he asked.

'The whole thing's wrong from the very beginning. There is no Rojo Pluma. You've already closed it, remember?'

'Yeah. But it's opening again. New name, new management.'

'There's the answer then. Keep it closed. You know what they say about avoiding temptation . . . the root of evil.'

'How does that help in getting' rid o' Newton Boe?'

'There'll be nothing for him to stay for. There won't be any shooting and he'll leave us alone. Mr Stearn won't have to fight him, and when him and Mrs Boe are gone, there'll be no more trouble.'

Henry looked at his daughter in a strange way, shocked by what she had to say. She seemed on the point of continuing her tirade, but Henry silenced her with a sharp wave of his hand. 'You can't see it, can you,' he said. 'This mornin' Clem Tapper was shot dead across the street, an' you're proposin' we turn the other goddamned cheek.'

'It seems to me he brought it on himself.'

'You're fast becoming a disappointment, Rose. If that's the way you think, you best take yourself home . . . stay away while I make an apology,' Henry rasped. 'Mrs Boe — with the help of Will Stearn — wants to run an honest establishment. Felix June can't cater for men who want entertainment after a high-stakes card game. An' cowboys on a three or four month cattle drive, gets a longin' for more than liquor, I can tell you. A place to let off steam's not always a sink o' corruption. You ought to think a little more about other folk an' their needs, maybe a lot less about yourself.'

Rose coloured instantly, stood there shaking her head. 'You've been blinded by her too,' she snapped, riled by her father's criticism.

'I certainly haven't seen what a spoiled little brat you've turned into. Now, get back to the house before I say somethin' we both regret.'

Rose backed off. She slowed when she reached the door, hoping he would call her back. But Henry had already turned away to fiddle with some pending circuit papers.

'That's the most speechifyin' I done since I took oath of office,' he muttered. 'As if I don't have enough trouble o' someone else's makin'.'

'But she is of your making,' Connie said tersely.

Henry stared back at her. 'What the hell do you know about it?'

'I know she's a kid who's been shouldering responsibilities beyond her years. Stuff she still doesn't understand. How long has she been without her mother?'

'Ten years,' Henry said, a little less irately. 'An' there's some things I don't need to be told. You think I don't know it's my fault?'

166

'No, I'm sure you do. I can't imagine anything worse than having to live with an irascible old mule, for all that time. No wonder the girl's confused. I'll go and talk to her.'

'You'll do no such thing, goddamnit. You keep away from her,' Henry barked out angrily.

'There you go, laying down the law again. Let her see and hear someone else besides you, for god's sake. While I'm doing *that*, maybe you can try to get my business back for me. The sooner we all do what we do best, the better it will be for everyone.' With that, Connie walked determinedly from the jailhouse.

Henry looked anxiously at Will who shrugged his shoulders. 'Don't look at me,' he offered. 'I know what I've got to do.'

'What the hell have we decided on?' Henry asked.

'You heard the lady. Except, as of a quarter hour ago, the business is hers *and* mine. How many men would you say could hold that place . . . from the inside?'

'Two. An' they're penned in like chute branders,' Henry said.

'Then you and me take the side door,' Will decided. 'If I make it, you won't be needed. If I don't, the commotion will at least give you a chance to get inside.'

'You know them doors ain't goin' to have welcome signs above 'em?'

'Yeah . . . the weak points of my plan. But you were the one for storming the joint, Sheriff. So let's go.'

# 15

Rose was near the Bighorn saloon when she stopped. She knew that to carry on, ignoring Connie Boe calling out her name, would only complicate matters. There were already some townsfolk watching, those who caught the whiff of trouble and collected accordingly. She lifted her head haughtily, didn't look around.

'I'd like to talk to you, Rose,' Connie started when she got close. 'It looks like now might be a good time.'

Rose stood back from her, unsure and still not saying anything.

'What I've got to say's not bad. I'm not out to corrupt you,' Connie continued. 'It's kind of obvious you can do with someone to talk to, and that's not something I suggest too often.'

'What could you possibly have to say that I would be interested in? 'Someone to talk to'?' Rose echoed incredulously. 'That's *you?*' She glared furiously at Connie, now. 'I'd say it's almost an offence to be sharing the same board-walk.'

'That's more sad than cruel, Rose, and uncalled for. We've probably got more in common than you think. Come on, let's go to the place I'm staying,' Connie replied in an almost friendly voice.

As if in no doubt that Rose would follow, Connie carried on along the boardwalk. She glanced at those about her, some who were openly staring. 'You'll catch wasps in there,' she said to one woman standing with her mouth agape. She went straight to the boarding-house and found the cook, asked him to bring coffee to the small lobby. 'Your gran'-mammy's quality,' she qualified. 'For two.'

A severely dressed townswoman with an empty marketing basket, brushed past Rose. 'I wouldn't get too close to her,' she said meanly. 'We all know what kind of woman she is . . . where she's been.'

Rose gave her a firm look. 'How?' she asked bluntly, sensing the reach of small-mindedness. She realized she didn't like the woman, decided to accept Connie Boe's invitation.

★ ★ ★

Connie asked Rose to sit down. She had chosen the lobby because it was more public, a kind of neutral territory. The two women sat thoughtfully, studying each other for a few seconds, before Connie spoke.

'When I was your age, I was married, hoping to raise a family,' she said. 'At the time we had no money and no prospects. Times were hard, very hard. We went without new clothing, proper meals, even.'

'Is that what all this is about?' Rose asked. 'You're looking for some sort of sympathy?'

'No, Rose, I left that behind a long

171

time ago . . . the day my husband rode off and left me. No, it's more how to wise up.'

Rose looked surprised. 'But your husband's *here*, in town. Newton Boe.'

'Yeah, that's him. He was once a stand-up guy, a real hombre. At least everybody thought he was. We had a section of land which he tried to work, but it was too much for him. So he rode off with a group of like-minded galoots to trade arms across the border. I didn't see him for two years, and by then I'd learned to live on my own. I had to give up the ranch, though, take the only work available for a young woman who's easy on the eye. I'd dance and spin till I'd faint, then I had to entertain the town's roughs and drunks.'

'Entertain them?' Rose queried with a wry twist of her mouth.

'Yeah. And let me tell you, Rose, it's not only roughs and drunks who have the monopoly on being rough and drunk. There's always a supposedly refined citizen who demands a certain kind of entertainment. But it was that or starve.'

'I think *I* might have starved. So what happened?'

'I was taking care of myself, staying clear of any real trouble. I'd got new friends, one in particular, when my husband turned up demanding all sorts of stuff.'

'And you let him have it?'

'As I said, there was someone *else*, but Newton threw him off the Honey Springs Bridge. I took to the road — the railroad to Alamosa, actually — and teamed up with a couple of other young runaways. We toured the silver mine camps, giving concerts. Ha, none of us could sing, but we knew the words and none of them old shovel-stiffs seemed to mind. There's a time and a place for everything, Rose, even looking good.'

As if taking in the sentiment of Connie's words, Rose was staring at the floor when the cook approached.

'Thank you,' Connie said. She waited for the man to leave, then poured their coffee. 'But you can probably guess what happened next,' she continued. 'He found me again, broke up our little sisterhood and took my last cent. And that's the story. As soon as I got settled, he'd crawl out of somewhere like a goddamn scorpion, kill any man who looked at me twice.'

'But now it's Ragland,' Rose remarked. '*That's* getting wise is it, to know that Will Stearn can expect the same fate?'

'He's going into business with me because it makes sense. And as far as my husband's force is concerned, the shoe's suddenly on the other foot, don't you think?'

Rose was becoming more bothered with every passing moment. 'So your purpose in siding with Will, is for him to rid you of Boe? You're using him.'

'No, Rose, I'm not. He's not a man to be used, and you know it. I came here and I liked what I saw . . . maybe we both did. I truly wanted to make another go of something. Later, when this is over, come to The Even Break and see for yourself. Soon, women will be demanding their own pleasures . . . a distraction from their dreary, humdrum lives. Visit us. I promise you won't be shocked or contaminated in any way.'

Rose finished her coffee and stood up. 'I'm sorry you've had such hard times here and elsewhere, Mrs Boe, but I'm afraid it doesn't change what I feel. My father has enough keeping-of-the-peace to do in this town, and I don't intend to see him burdened with any more. Don't you think that's fair, my wanting a less dangerous life for him?'

'It's fair. In fact it's not so different from what I want for me. I said we had something in common.'

Connie smiled weakly, indicated the way out and started towards the front door. 'You won't stop us, Rose. If my husband goes off in the meat wagon, I'll be staying on. Despite your fears, I do have new friends here. Friends who'll stand by me. And no one's going to suffer because of it.'

'Friends like Will Stearn. Except he

doesn't know the price,' Rose replied. 'Thank you for the coffee.'

Connie shook her head sadly, pushed the door to and leant against it. At that moment, if she had known another way out of her predicament she would have taken it. But there wasn't one. True to his nature, Newton Boe had trailed her to Ragland, even tried to rob her on the way. 'That's it, feller,' she muttered, determinedly. 'All that you've done just makes it easier.'

# 16

George Henry had deputized four men. Their faces were set grim, unsure of the danger from the windows of the Rojo Pluma.

Myles Brick watched what was going on from the safety of the bank premises. He had suggested his two clerks arm themselves. It wasn't part of their contract or part of any day's procedure, but it was accepted, readily understood that Brick wanted protection.

George Henry placed two of his men at opposite ends of the main street. If Newton Boe made good his escape from the Rojo Pluma, the sheriff didn't want him dead. He wanted him stopped and brought to justice, not to gather strength and return mob-handed. *Perhaps we should all retire to the Bighorn an' sit it out. Wait for the circuit judge,* he thought. *Kind of a shame it ain't my way*, as a wry afterthought.

The sun beat down stronger as the noon hour came and went. Now, nothing moved in the near-deserted street. The townsfolk trusted George Henry to do right by them. But in bogus confidence, many of them kept a motley assortment of side-arms within reach. Some of them thought they were ready to throw their weight behind Henry if he failed to hold the notorious Newton Boe.

Will was impatient to get into the fight. He was thinking of Clem Tapper, but he had given his word that he wouldn't make a move on his own without telling the sheriff. He would have gone on waiting if Connie Boe hadn't suddenly emerged from the boarding-house.

He immediately crossed the street, aware that in making his move he made an easy target. When no one took a pot-shot at him, he wondered if Plantin and Boe were still weighing-up the situation, thinking maybe they'd got it wrong.

'With due respect, ma'am, what the hell do you think you're doing?' Will said on reaching Connie, standing back from any line of fire.

Connie looked calmer than most other people in town, altogether assured. 'I'm going to call on Newt.'

'What for?'

'I don't know . . . don't suppose he will, either. But I've got to try something if I want to be a part of this town, Will.'

'He won't let you out again. He'll have got himself a hostage.'

Connie smiled forlornly. 'That was always my problem, wasn't it? At least if things don't turn out too well, you'll have yourself a full say in the business.'

Before Connie could make her move, George Henry came following in Will's footsteps across the street. Gasping and wiping sweat from his face, he asked Connie more-or-less the same question.

'Because, until an attorney says otherwise, I'm still his wife,' she said.

'You get yourself off this goddamn

street, lady, before I cart you off to one o' my cells. In there you can get spoony at nobody's expense.'

Connie looked solemnly at him for many heavy seconds before her neck muscles gave out and her head dropped.

Will saw her stub her toe into the boardwalk. Her chest heaved, and he knew she was close to tears.

Henry saw it too. 'I reckon now's a good a time as any,' he said. Then he turned back to face the side of the street opposite the Rojo Pluma, and yelled. 'OK men, put the fear o' hell-fire into 'em.'

'I've just been talking to someone who made it plain enough what the feeling of this town is . . . what they think of me. You could have let me try,' Connie said as two of the deputies opened up.

'That'll no doubt be my daughter. She's good at makin' her feelin's plain. But just because her an' some of her friends have got an opinion, it don't mean they're right,' Henry replied. 'So get yourself somewhere else. Make out a bill to the county ... claim against damage bein' done to your building.'

As Connie walked slowly away, Henry stood just off the boardwalk and watched the deputies' rifle bullets smash at the façade of the Rojo Pluma. *There's a time for makin' sacrifices lady, an' a time for not*, he told himself.

'Now go for your side door,' he shouted, turning to Will. 'We're soft-enin' 'em up for you.'

'Right. You stay here,' Will snapped. 'I don't intend to run a business in a town without proper law.'

'Sorry, I've got somewhere else to be.'

'Where the hell's that?'

'The front, goddamnit. Bein' bold's half a battle.'

Taking a diagonal run across the street, Henry stumbled forward. With one good arm, he was firing and levering bullets into his carbine, the measured broadside from his deputies ceasing for a moment.

Will cursed and cursed. Other than a misplaced obligation, he had no idea why Henry should be risking his life. He raised his hand. In the light of no retaliation he hoped it would signal the sheriff's deputies to hang fire again. Knowing there was little chance of catching a bullet unless Boe or Plantin emerged from the building through the side door, he ran straight for the Rojo Pluma.

At the corner of the alley he stopped, used the eerie silence to listen for any giveaway sounds. He drew his Colt, set the action and went forward. A figure appeared from back in the alley and he stepped quickly to clapboards of the building almost opposite the side door of the Rojo Pluma.

'There shouldn't be anything but refuse bins and beer piss, back there,' he called out. 'If you want to live, keep on coming . . . real slow. How the hell did *you* get here?' he then rasped out as Owen Hunston sidled towards him in the building's thin shadow.

'I got away. Boe's turnin' real mad.'

'You got away? How?'

Hunston nodded at the side door. 'I was supposed to be makin' a barricade. I fooled him into thinkin' I was with him. He was watchin' me like a hawk, all night. Him an' Plantin. I made a break for it this mornin' when he was cuttin' down Clem Tapper. I've been back there among the bins . . . waitin'. You know Rook's dead?'

'Of course I know.' Will let his temperament settle with a few deep breaths, then motioned Hunston to come forward. 'So if Boe thought you were with him, you'll know what he's plannin' to do,' he said. 'Lie to me, and you'll be begging for mercy. Do you understand?'

'Yeah. He's goin' to fight it out. He's beyond any reason . . . sees Ragland as some sort o' last stand.'

'And Plantin's sticking with him?'

Hunston made a thin, sly smile. 'He don't have much choice. If he had, he'd be here with me or on the way out o' town. But he's too close. He knows if he even sneezes wrong, Boe will shoot him dead.'

'How do we get in there?'

'You don't. Not front or back. You'd need a batterin' ram.'

'What about here?' Will indicated the side door.

Hunston offered a shrug. 'I think it's open, makes it the only place they have to watch. There is a window beside the back door. It's very narrow. I guess no one's supposed to come through there.'

Will turned when he saw that Hunston had seen something behind him. He went into a near crouch, stood again at George Henry's approach.

'Hah, my diversionary tactic,' the sheriff said, breathlessly. 'They'll be busy thinkin' we're shootin' out the front o' the building. Let's get 'em through here.'

'No,' Will replied. 'We don't know enough. According to Hunston, that's what they're waiting for. But there's a window at the back, apparently. It should at least get me in.'

'Yeah, but gettin' out's your trouble,' Henry commented, then: 'Where'd you crawl from?' when he saw Hunston. 'There's no stones big enough down here.'

Hunston didn't answer, just looked around as if considering the last part of his escape.

'Get out,' Will told him. 'Go to the jailhouse, and wait there. Find your real boss. Maybe she'll appreciate your story.'

# 17

'Let's go find this goddamn window,'
Henry rasped, setting off down the
alleyway towards the back of the building. He was level with the side door
when it opened a few inches. In one
swift movement he swung his carbine
around and fired. The bullet shattered
the door panelling a fraction of a second
behind where Hoke Plantin's startled
face had been.

Close behind, Will made an instant
decision. Knowing there was little
chance of entering through the back of
the building, he jammed his boot heel
into the dirt for leverage, twisted
sideways and hurled himself, shoulder
first, at the door. As the panels split, he
shielded his face in the crook of his left
arm, toppled off balance through the
broken gap and landed heavily inside.
He gasped, rolled to one side as bullets

zipped around him.

Cursing with resolve, he dived for a table, pulling down a big plush curtain that was screening the covert gambling room off to one side. Through the crash of more gunfire he heard what he thought was George Henry breaking through the rear window. He hunkered down, pulling over the table as cover, alert for a more precise direction of the shots. It was Boe or Plantin shooting at him, maybe both, but he knew they didn't have a direct sighting, only that he'd come through the side door. He took a guess that Boe would be somewhere near the front of the building, that Plantin probably only had time to find cover beyond the gambling room, maybe somewhere among the gaming tables. He manoeuvred into a sitting position, held his Colt in both hands and waited for one of them to make a move.

Plantin rose cautiously above one of the tables. Will's fast shot crashed through the chuck-a-luck cage, sent it spinning, its dice flying across the room. The big gunman had Will to his left, Boe to his right and was in fear of them both. With the quarry's fear of being trapped, he took a startled look around him, ran low towards the rear of the building.

Boe saw him, without any warning, fired. The bullet ripped through the side of Plantin's jacket, tight under his arm. The impact made him drop his gun, brought him to his knees.

'So help me Hoke, you run, an' I'll kill you an' him both,' Boe rasped out.

Plantin stayed low, very still, not knowing who or what to fear most. But death won out, and with the gut feeling of knowing he was about to die, he made a fateful lunge for the show stage. 'I'll give you a goddamn performance,' he yelled. 'You an' your cursed spouse.'

Boe stood with his legs apart, steadied himself and fired. 'From me an' Miss Connie,' he announced as Plantin caught the bullet in his chest. Plantin took one step forward then turned around, presented Boe with his back. A second bullet smashed through the front of the piano and a twang erupted from inside. Boe's third shot hammered hard between Plantin's shoulder blades. The man sighed as he went down, but with the power of those whose big bodies protect them, he straightened again and tried to remain on his feet. As he finally lost balance, there was no more sound from him and he fell headlong across the piano keyboard. His meaty hands smashed down on to the keys, and in his moment of dying he grinned pitifully. Banging out a few notes on a piano was something he had always wanted to do.

'You really are a son-of-a-bitch,' Will said quietly. 'But I guess three was a crowd.' On Boe's firing, he had moved from cover to watch the exchange. He would have killed Plantin himself given the chance, but not with a backshot.

A bullet ripped out a chunk of top edge of the overturned table. Will turned sideways, held out his gun hand

and fired three fast shots at Boe, heard a hard-bitten curse as he stepped back.

'Not good enough, Stearn. You want to come see?' Boe shouted.

A bullet awaited Will if he risked responding to Boe's taunting offer, so he didn't move, except to refill the cylinder of his Colt.

The shooting from the street petered out and Will thought it might be the deputies trying to determine what was happening inside the Rojo Pluma. He wasn't sure how many times Boe had fired, but guessed the man would be carrying more than one Colt.

'It won't work, Boe,' he returned. 'If you nail me, they'll flush you from cover like a plump quail. Me and Connie are the partners now. She'll burn the place down with you inside.' Will laughed to himself at the chance of Boe yielding. He knew there was going to be no surrender.

As Will expected, nothing happened. The only movement which disturbed the relentless silence was off to his right. He turned to see George Henry pulling himself through the narrow window at the rear of the building. Will cursed and yelled for him to get back, but it was of no use. The old sheriff wriggled himself awkwardly and painfully through the frame, and dropped to the floor.

Newton Boe's next bullet thumped into the window frame an inch from Henry's ear. But the man steadied himself, hung on to his faithful carbine and stared eagerly around the room.

'That's the other way in,' Will muttered. Once again he turned sideways, held out his gun hand and fired two even shots at Boe. The echo of the shots was still reverberating around the room as Henry crawled into the cover of the bulky table.

'Welcome. Real lawman's thinking,' Will said drily.

Henry was catching his breath. 'Boe's cornered,' he gasped.

'Yeah, I know. It's what I'm worried about.'

'You come at him from the right,' Henry suggested. 'I'll stay here an' keep him busy. He won't be able to take us both down.'

Will gave Henry a doubtful look. *Yeah, I know that as well*, he thought. 'I'll try to get closer to that stage,' he said. 'It's where he shot Plantin. So if he had a sighting, it makes him vulnerable.'

*This is how Plantin must've felt, 'cept there weren't anyone to side him*, Henry thought as Will ran from their cover.

Immediately, Boe attempted to cut Will down, was taking aim when Henry's indiscriminate covering fire stopped him. He swung around, fired off a brace of shots before returning his attention to Will. But by then the distraction had worked, he was a second or two too late. He fired out of anger, and the bullet smashed into the glass front of a small drinks bar as Will dodged down behind it.

A silence settled now between the

three of them. Sour gunsmoke hung low, barely moving in the sudden stillness of the room.

Henry reloaded his carbine, ran the situation over in his mind. 'Hey,' he shouted to Will. 'At Fredericksburg, me an' a rifleman got behind a big apple barrel to roll up on Johnny Reb. Can you move that piano?'

'Right now I don't have your connections, Sheriff, and this is not Fredericksburg.'

At the exchange between Will and the sheriff, sweat glistened across Boe's sallow cheekbones. He fired into the bar once again and cursed. Then to one side, he saw the bulky gaming table rolling slowly on its edge across the floor towards him.

'Hey, Stearn. If this ever makes a newspaper, make sure it's the funnies section,' Boe called out. 'Notorious gunslinger in shoot-out with chuck-a-luck table, should have 'em die laughin'.'

'No one else is dyin' at your expense,

Boe,' Henry rasped back. 'You're through.'

'You keep your nose out of it,' Boe continued. 'Stearn, are you listenin'? It's you an' me if you're up to it.'

'I'm ready,' Will agreed. 'It's your choosing.'

'I'm still the goddamn sheriff o' this town,' Henry retaliated angrily. 'I'd rather trust a sidewinder, than you, Boe. Clem Tapper, Rook an' Plantin are all dead by your hand. Them's the last.'

'Gun's in my holster, Sheriff. If you want an easy kill.'

'Wrong time to push me, Boe. I'll shoot you any way I can for the greater good.'

Boe took a couple of deep breaths, doubled his leg up and placed the flat of his boot against the wall behind him. His spare features twisted into a sardonic grin as he peered through the acrid, cordite-smoked room. 'OK, I've considered what you have to say, Sheriff.' As he spoke, Boe kicked himself forward from the trap he'd let them get him into. His gun exploded in his fist, his bullets whipping first for Henry and then for Will.

Will opened fire to match Boe. For the briefest moment he held the man's face in his sights. It was all he needed for a single, stopping shot.

Boe was standing upright and very still when the second bullet hit him. 'As I was tellin' you, I'm still Sheriff,' George Henry rasped out. 'Lord knows for how much longer,' he added tiredly.

But Boe didn't go down. He stood for a moment, as if turned to stone. Then with his chest broken and bloody, he toppled forward, fired one more time into the puncheons at his feet.

'Weren't that good with a gun, was he?' Henry mumbled.

'You don't have to be,' Will replied. 'You just do things with it that others won't.'

# 18

For the second time since arriving in Ragland, Will Stearn attended a burial. It was late afternoon and Connie Boe stood by the grave-side. Her head was bowed, but it was for her own thoughts. 'I'll see someone about a headstone,' she murmured after the final shovelful of earth was thrown. 'I said it would be the last thing he ever got from me. I'll keep my word on that, if nothing else.' Then, with a detached look she made her way back to the town.

George Henry went across to Will, nodded curtly to emphasize his satisfaction with the brief service. He grimaced at pains in his shoulder and across his rib area.

'I could make good use of a drink,' he suggested five minutes later as they approached the jailhouse.

'Medicinal reasons?' Will asked.

'Nope.'

Felix June handed over two glasses and a bottle of Old Crow. He had things to say to Will, concerning Clem Tapper, but he moved off along the counter to let the two men talk.

'What now?' Henry asked after an appreciative few sips of his whiskey.

'Seems you keep asking me that,' Will replied with a friendly smile. 'I hear the old Rojo Pluma got shot to pieces. So bad it got itself closed down.'

'Yeah, for the second time.' Henry returned the smile and raised his glass in salute. 'But it's re-openin'. Word says, tonight.'

'Well, I never heard that.' Will finished his drink, nodded to June and went out. He walked the street, stood for a moment in the last of the day's light before entering the bullet-riddled establishment.

Connie Boe was directing workmen in making good from the gun-fight. She walked over to Will with Owen Hunston beside her. 'Owen forgot his allegiance for a while . . . what side his bread was buttered,' she said with a half-smile. 'What do you say, partner?'

'I guess we all get forgetful sometime.'

'Thanks,' Hunston said. 'From now on, who do I answer too?'

'You work for us both . . . the answer's there somewhere,' Connie said. 'We're opening tonight. You know what needs doing. Will, do you want to move your stuff in upstairs? I could send somebody to collect.'

Will frowned, shook his head at the offer. 'I hadn't figured on opening tonight. Bit soon isn't it?'

Connie shook her head. 'Never. We're going to take a pile of money in the coming months. There's cowboy dollars coming in from the cattle drives, and the spur line's going to be dropping plump, rich customers at our doorstep. I'll want a couple of men here most, if not all of the time. And preferably married ones.'

'Why married?'

'I'm likely to get ideas . . . find my mind wandering away from business. The new Connie Moss doesn't aim to wither on the vine, young feller.'

Will grinned, flexed his shoulders uneasily. 'Yeah, there was something I meant to ask you along those lines,' he started, but Connie pushed him away.

'Go and get your traps,' she said. 'Remember I don't want any shadows falling over tonight's opening. It's a fandango for some of us lucky folk, so get yourself cleaned up as well.'

Will went to his room at the boarding-house. He shut the door, lay full stretch on the bed, put his head back and closed his eyes. He had a few minutes wondering who Connie's lucky folk might be, then a few more, thinking about one or two unresolved problems. An hour later, he swung his legs down and packed his gear, such as it was. In quick order, he had a bath, dressed in the only change of clothing he'd got, and carried his saddle-bag down to the street.

George Henry had been waiting outside on a boardwalk bench. Like Will he had changed from his work clothes. 'So it is tonight then?' he said. 'I weren't too sure on account o' not havin' an invitation. But I figured on me bein' an elected town officer, an' all, I didn't need one. Would o' been nice though, a sign of appreciation.'

Will studied him carefully. 'If you've finished. I'm a joint owner and I haven't got an invite, either. Fact is, I didn't know we were in business till little more than an hour ago. But we're certainly not wasting a good wash n' brush up, are we, Sheriff?'

'Or these go-to-meeting duds. Meantime, I'm headed home. I don't trust much outside cookin' in Ragland.'

'Yeah, that could be some of my unfinished business . . . something for me to take care of.'

'Call for me, why don't you?' the sheriff suggested. 'We'll go for a more dignified entrance than last time,' he added.

Will wondered why Henry hadn't invited him back for a meal, thought he probably knew the answer. Along the main street, he was surprised to be acknowledged by almost every person that passed . . . even some of the womenfolk. *It's probably getting rid of someone worse than me*, he thought.

Owen Hunston was waiting for him. 'Your room's at the back. It's got one o' them fanlight windows, but it ain't too noisy,' he said and took Will's bag.

Will walked through the big room which Connie had so hastily but decoratively dressed a week ago. Apart from the chuck-a-luck table, the small drinks bar with its smashed glass, and a dozen or so bullet holes, the place was almost fixed. Someone was knocking out a few discordant notes, on the shattered piano, and Will went over to have a word.

'It's already had one professional have a go at it,' he said.

'You're Will Stearn, aren't you?' the man said without looking up.

'Yeah. Who are you?'

'Eli Peglar. I came in on the stage earlier. So you're calling yourself a professional, are you?'

Will got close to a laugh, took a fast liking to the man. 'No, it wasn't me. I was the one hiding behind it.'

'Well it needs more work than I can handle. I just play the thing. It should be OK for simple tunes, though.'

Will was about to ask, 'Like what?' when Connie came rushing up. She took Will by the arm and led him directly to the front door.

'After all that's happened, we really should have the sheriff here,' she said. 'A lot of it's down to him . . . the fact we're actually welcoming folk back. But he's still living in the bygones and wants to be invited proper. Why not go and make it personal?'

Will felt there was something wrong, but he couldn't put his finger on it, and before he could put together a question, Connie had him out of the door, under the newly painted 'The Even Break' sign and into the street. For a minute or so he stood enjoying the quiet and coolness of twilight, then he made his way through town to the sheriff's house.

George Henry had asked him to call, but as Will brushed the hibiscus, he again felt the misgivings. He wanted this night to run smoothly, didn't need Rose Henry's scorn, the tirade they suffered in the jailhouse.

⋆　⋆　⋆

He rapped the front door and George Henry arrived quickly. So quickly, Will knew he must have been keeping an eye out for him.

'I guess you're more important than you think,' Will said. 'Not many get a messenger with a personal invite from Connie Boe herself.'

'Her idea?' Henry wanted to know.

'Yeah. I never said a word.'

'Good. That's real good. Come on in.'

'I hadn't reckoned on hanging

around. Perhaps we should make a move,' Will stalled.

'Nothing's goin' to happen till we get there.' Henry indicated for Will to step inside the house. 'Wait here a sec, there's somethin' you should see,' he said, and went off hurriedly. Will walked into the front parlour, looked around at the comfortable furnishings, felt a curious sensation of loneliness. He was deep in thought, peering at a photographic portrait of someone he thought might have been Rose's mother, when Rose herself came into the room.

Her blue dress was simply decorated and longer than usual. With her raven hair hanging loose, she upheld Will's opinion of being the most attractive girl he'd seen for a very long time, if not ever. She stopped and gasped in surprise, and he suddenly felt very awkward and out of place.

'Your pa said there was something for me to see. Obviously, he didn't let you in on it. For that, I'm sorry,' he apologized quickly.

Rose nodded. 'It's OK. We must allow him a bit of fun now and again. It doesn't happen that often. I'm his escort for the opening tonight . . . *your* opening night. So shouldn't you be there, organizing or something.'

'No. We hire people for all that. Well, I hope we do. His escort, did you say?'

'He wants an aide, someone to stop him spending too much time at the punch bowl. It's the sort of offer a girl finds hard to refuse.'

Will, feeling heat rise in his face, went on looking at her. He wanted to ask how difficult it would be to refuse an invitation from him, but he knew his voice wouldn't convert the thought accurately enough.

A moment later Henry came back into the room. He looked from one to the other. 'I went to the trouble o' gettin' you two together, an' all you can do is talk about *me*.'

'Perhaps if you'd told us, we could have had a say in the matter,' Rose retaliated.

'Yeah, I can imagine. Well, I'm cuttin' along to the party.' Henry patted the pockets of his coat as though checking on his chattels, then he closed the door tellingly behind him.

Will was going to question him, but changed his mind. 'I knew there was something up. They were in cahoots,' he said to Rose.

'Who were?'

'Connie Boe and your pa.'

'Yes. Thinking back, I think you're right. We've been cozened.'

This was the time to say it, Will knew. He couldn't let the opportunity slide away for the want of directness. 'In some parts of town, I'm already considered to be a man of integrity and decent temperament. So, bearing that in mind, and the game your pa and Miss Connie are playing, what if I was to ask you to accompany *me*?' he said.

'Playing games isn't for me, Will. But I sort of like the idea of it. I guess there's a lot of learning for me.'

'No, not so much, Rose. It's more a

case of clearing out other folks' narrow-mindedness. But that's nothing a couple of hours dancing can't put right.'

We do hope that you have enjoyed
reading this large print book.

Did you know that all of our titles
are available for purchase?

We publish a wide range of high
quality large print books including:
**Romances, Mysteries, Classics**
**General Fiction**
**Non Fiction and Westerns**

Special interest titles available in
large print are:
**The Little Oxford Dictionary**
**Music Book, Song Book**
**Hymn Book, Service Book**

Also available from us courtesy of
Oxford University Press:
**Young Readers' Dictionary**
**(large print edition)**
**Young Readers' Thesaurus**
**(large print edition)**

For further information or a free
brochure, please contact us at:
**Ulverscroft Large Print Books Ltd.,**
**The Green, Bradgate Road, Anstey,**
**Leicester, LE7 7FU, England.**
**Tel:** (00 44) **0116 236 4325**
**Fax:** (00 44) **0116 234 0205**

# SAVAGE

## Jake Henry

In 1864, Captain Jeff Savage is tasked with taking down Carver's Raiders, a ruthless bunch of killers who have blasted a bloody path through the Shenandoah Valley. The mission is a failure, and Carver escapes with a handful of men. Two years later, he and his gang rob a bank in Summerton, murdering Savage's wife Amy. Several outlaws escape in the aftermath: armed with their names, Savage sets out to track each one down and exact his revenge . . .